SO PUNK ROCK

To the memory of our grandparents Mortimer and Miriam Ostow, whose lives and work showed us that adherence to tradition and the questioning of boundaries are not mutually exclusive. We think they would have dug this book, when all was said and done.

SO PUNK ROCK

(And Other Ways to Disappoint Your Mother)

A Novel by Micol Ostow

Art by DAvid Ostow

Woodbury, Minnesota

First Edition
First Printing, 2009

Book design by Steffani Sawyer
Cover design by Lisa Novak
Cover images:
© 2009 Artville—Weathered Backgrounds (2 banners)
© 2009 Image 100—Party (crowd at top)
© 2009 Digital Stock—Arts & Entertainment (lights behind crowd at the top)
Art © 2009 David Ostow

Flux, an imprint of Llewellyn Publications

Library of Congress Cataloging-in-Publication Data
Ostow, Micol.
So punk rock (and other ways to disappoint your mother) : a novel / by Micol Ostow; with art by David Ostow.—1st ed.
p. cm.
Summary: Four suburban New Jersey students from the Leo R. Gittleman Jewish Day School form a rock band that becomes inexplicably popular, creating exhiliration, friction, confrontation, and soul-searching among its members.
ISBN 978-0-7387-1471-4
[1. Rock groups—Fiction. 2. Jews—United States—Fiction. 3. Interpersonal relations—Fiction. 4. High schools—Fiction. 5. Schools—Fiction. 6. New Jersey—Fiction.] I. Ostow, David, 1979– ill. II. Title.
PZ7.O8475So 2009
[Fic]—dc22
2009008216

Flux
Llewellyn Publications
A Division of Llewellyn Worldwide, Ltd.
2143 Wooddale Drive, Dept. 978-0-7387-1471-4
Woodbury, MN 55125-2989, U.S.A.
www.fluxnow.com

Printed in the United States of America

Acknowledgements

MICOL would like to thank Jodi Reamer, for (pun fully intended) keeping the faith; Carrie Jones for the good old-fashioned shidduch; Andrew Karre, Brian Farrey, Sandy Sullivan, Courtney Kish, and the rest of the fab team at Flux, who are all totally punk rock; Mom, Dad, and all of the Ostows (who've proven shockingly impervious to disappointment, even when I told them I was leaving my day job to write full-time); Noah, who is even more brilliant and creative than Ari; the students and faculty of Solomon Schechter Day School of Essex and Union, for obvious reasons; and the wonderful community at Vermont College of the Fine Arts, in particular Kathi Appelt, David Gifaldi, Sharon Darrow, Ellen Howard, Uma Krisnaswami, Tim Wynne-Jones, and Louise Hawes.

Oh—and David, for having all of the good ideas. And for being nothing like Ben. Rock on, little brother.

DAVID would like to thank Micol, to whose talent and ambition all of this book's success is due; Jodi Reamer, for her enthusiasm and her apparently cavalier attitude toward flat-out nepotism; the Flux team: Andrew, Brian, Courtney, Sandy, and especially Lynne, Lisa, and Jeanette for making the book beautiful and my art presentable; Tracy Eisenberg, whose positive outlook rubs off on me more than I let on; Dan Salomon, the yin to my yang and sometimes vice versa, for his hard work on the book trailer; my parents, whose example it has been and will always be my life's work to follow; Tom Burns and his Kimballs and Tracy and Frank's Possessions for rocking and/or rolling me as circumstances called for over the past year; all of the teachers who saw me through thirteen years of Jewish schooling and who—without my realizing it—instilled within me a sense of identity that's both grounded me and set me spinning amidst the myriad frustrating yet fascinating questions involving what it means to be a Jew; and of course all the kids who went down this path with me who, in their differences, make the questions that much more complex and the answers that much more satisfyingly elusive.

. . . and in my going out to meet you,
I found you coming toward me.
—Yehuda ha-Levi

PSSST!!!.....

KID, YOU HAVE NO IDEA WHERE YOU ARE OR WHERE YOU'RE GOING. ARE YOU REALLY IN A PLACE TO BE ASKING QUESTIONS?

YOU DO RAISE A GOOD POINT, MYSTERIOUS STRANGER. YOUR SPINE-TINGLINGLY GRUFF VOICE SOUNDS TO BE COMING FROM THE ABANDONED, UNLIT ALLEY AT THE END OF THE BLOCK. I'LL BE RIGHT OVER...

I WAS 12 YEARS OLD THE FIRST TIME I EVER FELT ROBBED BY MY COMMITMENT TO JUDAISM...
NITE
HAND OVER THE GELT, KID, AND NOBODY GETS HURT.
I THINK I HEAR SIRENS, GUYS! OH MAN, THIS WAS A BAD IDEA! GAME OVER, MAN, WE'RE TOAST!
OH GOD, EUGENE, NOW IS NOT THE TIME FOR ONE OF YOUR FREAK-OUTS!
QUIET, THE BOTH OF YEZ!
dko '07

IT WAS EREV YOM KIPPUR, THE HOLIEST NIGHT OF THE YEAR...

THE OLD TIMERS

THE UPSTARTS

THE URBANITES

THE SUBURBANITES

THE JOCKS

THE GEEKS

THE OBSERVANT

THE NOT-SO-OBSERVANT

• • •

OF COURSE MY PARENTS WOULDN'T LET ME GO...

ALL THROUGH THE SYNAGOGUE SERVICE THE ONLY THING I COULD THINK ABOUT WAS HOW MUCH FUN CHRIS MUST BE HAVING AT THE SHOW.

CHRIS

CHRIS' MOM

MY PARENTS HAD NO IDEA. THEY HAD THEIR OWN THOUGHTS ABOUT **THEIR** RELIGION THAT THEY WERE DETERMINED TO FOIST ON **ME**.

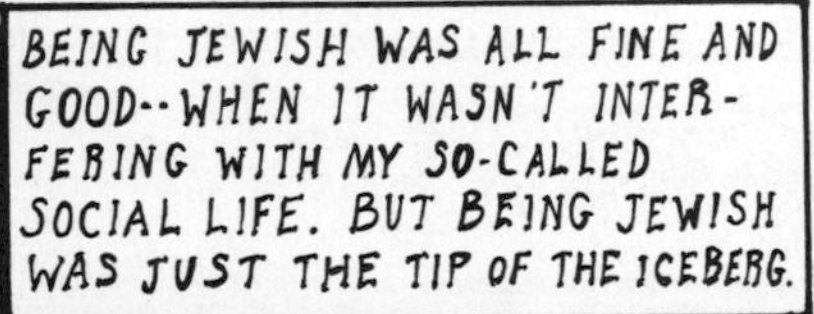

JUDAISM WAS ONE TINY CORNERSTONE OF MY IDENTITY. BUT I HAD A HIGHER CALLING, ONE THAT NO PARENT, NO RABBI, NO PROPHET, NO ANGEL COULD EVEN BEGIN TO GRASP. . .

* EVENTUALLY. SO FAR I OWNED THE SUNGLASSES (A CHUCK E CHEESE PARTY FAVOR) AND THE TATTOOS (TEMPORARY AND WATER-SOLUBLE). ROCKSTARDOM WAS A GUITAR, AN AMP AND 7000 SCREAMING FANS AWAY.

one

There are many things that Jonas Fein does well.

For instance, he's awesome at coming up with plausible stories on the spot that will placate even the most suspicious of parents and the most stern of teachers. He's a virtuoso of the hackneyed excuse: I've seen him feed his homework to his dog, self-induce flu-like symptoms, and excuse himself from final exams to rescue nonexistent puppies from imaginary fires. But mostly he gets by with his smile. If there's a cute girl or whatever that you want to talk to, but you're, like, feeling shy, Jonas has no qualms whatsoever about going up to her and breaking the ice.

You just have to be sure that you're okay with that. Jonas' ice-breaking, that is. Because once he pulls out his fail-safe "who, me?" grin, your chances with said girl may be toast. She may be lost forever to the cult of the Fein.

Are you jealous? Don't be. Jonas is charming. He just is. That's his thing.

My thing? I'm Ari Abramson, and my thing is that I'm Jonas' best friend.

I've been his best friend since the third grade, when we both played defense in the B'nai Brith soccer league. Jonas was better than I was, but that didn't keep us from hanging out together. And we stayed tight, all throughout elementary school and on through junior high.

Now that we're both officially juniors at Leo R. Gittleman Jewish Day School, it would appear that Jonas needs me more than ever. After all, every alpha dog needs a beta, right? That's me: beta.

Therefore, it's my job to break it to Jonas that while he has certainly mastered the art of getting away with just about anything, and that he does have many totally appealing talents and strengths... well, singing is just not one of them.

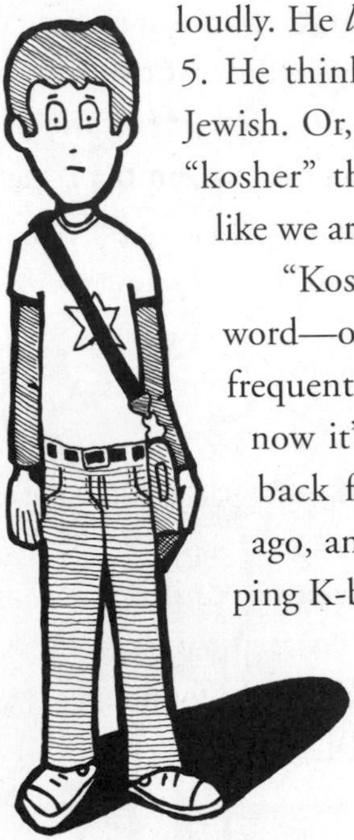

Singing is what he is doing now, and loudly. He *loves* the new single from Maroon 5. He thinks it's cool that Adam Levine is Jewish. Or, excuse me, *kosher.* He thinks it's "kosher" that Adam Levine is Jewish. Just like we are.

"Kosher" is slang. I mean, it's a real word—one that gets tossed around pretty frequently at Gittleman—but apparently now it's all reappropriated. Jonas came back from Camp Habonim six weeks ago, and ever since then he's been dropping K-bombs right and left.

"*Everybody* says it at Habonim," he informed me, the first time he tried it out on me and I looked at him, puzzled.

I didn't doubt him. And besides, if Jonas Fein is using the expression, it won't be long before *everybody* at Gittleman is saying it, too.

But I digress. At this precise moment, Jonas is engaged in what he clearly

NAME: ARI SAMUEL ABRAMSON
DATE OF BIRTH: MARCH 30, 1993
HEIGHT: 5'-9"
ACTIVITIES: SAT PREP
BABYSITTING
INTERESTS: DOODLING, CARAMEL MACCHIATOS, MUSIC, MUSIC, MUSIC
KNOWN TO SAY: "IT'S KIND OF POST-STOOGES ERA IGGY MEETS EARLY SPRINGSTEEN WITH A TOUCH OF CLASH AND COME ON PILGRIM ERA PIXIES PRODUCTION QUALITY... YOU'D LIKE IT!"

considers to be singing. I myself would beg to differ. And also, he's throwing me off my game. It's hard to focus when one is being serenaded by dulcet croonings not unlike the noise a cat might make, if said cat were, somehow, simultaneously in heat and dying. I've lost the first two rounds of Mario Kart, and I'm pretty sure I'm seconds away from wiping out for good. I concentrate instead on the sound of the washing machine coming from the basement in a futile effort to focus. I think it's on rinse cycle two; I'm used to this exercise.

"Ha!" Jonas laughs. "You're f^&*ing done, man." He tosses his controller toward the television.

I glance at my watch. "My mom'll be here in a minute, anyway."

"You're not staying to eat?" Jonas asks, surprised. Jonas' mother is extremely trigger-happy when it comes to ordering pizza and for that reason, I can often be found crashing the Feins' dinner table.

"Nah," I say. "Homework."

"Dude, we've barely been in school a week," Jonas obviouses. "What f^&*ing homework do you have?"

"I have to finish covering my books" I say. I try for sarcastic, but Jonas can read me like a back issue of *Spin.* Covered books is something my parents bug me about at the beginning of every school year. They have strange ideas about academic priorities.

"Dude, let me f^&*ing do that for you tomorrow in homeroom. It'll take me two seconds."

The offer is tempting, but I know better. The last time I took Jonas up on this suggestion he returned to me a set of books plastered with stickers featuring slogans that ranged from the political (*Skateboarding is not a Crime*) to the ironic (*My Child is an Honor Student at Leo R. Gittleman High School*) to the simply inappropriate (*Porn Star*). Needless to say this is not exactly what my parents, teachers, and other various authority figures have in mind, so I decline and change the subject.

"Anyway, my parents want me to take a practice SAT."

Jonas looks at me like I have seven heads. "They do realize that the SATs aren't until forever from now, right?"

"Yes."

"And that you're registered for a prep course?"

"Yes."

"And that these scores don't even count, unless they're, like, amazing? That we're just boning up for next year? When we're all going to take them again?"

Obvious, obvious, obvious.

"Yes."

"Dude." He shrugs. "F^&*."

There's really not much else to be said.

"*Obviously,* they're a little high-strung," I agree.

"It's ridiculous. You're not going to have a problem getting into Brandeis," Jonas says.

Brandeis is where my parents met. They have decided that it would be the perfect college for me. I suspect that they may have actually decided this before I was even born. Supposedly something like 47 percent of all Gittleman grads go on to study at Brandeis. Which makes it perhaps not the most diverse collegiate experience I could possibly have.

In case you haven't guessed, I'm not sure I'm interested in going to Brandeis. I'm trying—was trying all summer, in fact—to think about how to break this news to my parents. I haven't come up with much, inspiration-wise. Camp Ramah wasn't totally conducive to brainstorming. Mindy Jacobs *finally* started wearing a bra—the realization of which took up most of my bunk's emotional energy.

From outside, I hear a car horn honking. Two short, quick consecutive blasts—mom's signature honk.

Jonas nods. "F^&*, man. Right on schedule."

"Duh." My parents are extremely fond of their schedules.

Jonas smirks at me by way of reply. With a sudden burst of energy, he leaps into the air and breaks out into an impromptu air guitar, singing along in his best Adam Levine.

I wince. Dying, heated cats.

Jonas is going to have to practice, I realize, as I make my way downstairs, out the door, and into my mother's appallingly suburban SUV. She kisses me on the cheek and I furtively check the rearview mirror for lipstick stains. I feel as if I can still hear him caterwauling even through the walls of the house. Jonas is going to have to learn to sing.

Like, sing *well.*

See, I've got a sort of a plan for junior year. But I'm going to need Jonas' help in order to put it into action.

And even with Jonas—even with Jonas singing with the grace and the nuance of a choirboy—even then, it's still a long shot.

But I have to try.

• • •

My parents' love of all things scheduled extends to dinner, which is held at 7:00 PM sharp on weekdays (though they have been known to play it fast and loose on Saturday nights, if they've been tipping into the Manischewitz). While Jonas surely scarfs down slice after grease-soaked slice of pepperoni pizza over at Casa Fein, I poke half-heartedly at some "unfried" chicken and a pile of broccoli that's been steamed to a nearly unrecognizable mush. If only my parents weren't so actively anti–fast food. Or even slower food that tasted good. Yeah, I'd take that.

"Ari, that's disgusting."

At first I think my mom means the broccoli. Although surprising coming from her, this is a point I am willing to concede. It quickly dawns on me, though, that she means the little mound of vegetable-puree that I've created in the center of my plate.

"Sorry." I rake my fork across my plate in what I hope is a convincing pantomime of eating. I shovel some chicken into my mouth and wash it down with a swig of Coke. Yum.

My mother shakes her head in a "kids today" sort of way. Like I'm completely insane for preferring the deep-fried food groups to anything organic. It's been too long since she's eaten chicken fingers or nachos; she's lost her perspective on reality. She should spend some time in the Gittleman lunchroom-slash-assembly space.

On second thought, maybe not. I shudder. She'd *love* that. She would be a PTA Lunch Committee renegade. Bad idea. *Horrible,* hideous idea. Scratch that. I cough and take another sip of soda.

"*Chew.*" She takes an exaggerated bite, brandishing her knife and fork like musical instruments. In other words, I am a cretin. I can't help it. I eat at the speed of sound. Even when it's . . . *organic.*

My brother Ben, who sits to my mother's left, picks up his utensils and launches into his own demonstration of *The Complete Idiot's Guide to Table Manners*. Ben is eleven, and a parent's dream, which equals about twenty-three different kinds of annoying to me. He is one of those types who actually prefers steamed vegetables to Chicken McNuggets. I hope it's just that he doesn't know any better because really, it's not natural. He smiles beatifically at me and swallows, resting his cutlery against his plate again between bites.

"You have broccoli on your chin." I point with the tip of my knife.

(He doesn't.)

"Do not." But he rubs at it vigorously nonetheless.

"So." My father breaks the brief silence, then pauses

as though unsure of where to take the platform he's just commandeered. He regards his napkin thoughtfully. "So," he repeats, trying again, "what did you and Jonas get up to this afternoon?"

Oh. *This* conversation. I know this conversation well, can tell you exactly where it's going. I wish there were a set of acronyms or something, like you have online, so we could shorthand the whole unpleasantness.

"Video games," I say cautiously. "World domination. Cheez-Its. You know."

"Any studying?"

"Well—" How to put this delicately? "Jonas and I aren't in too many of the same classes." This is a piece of information that consistently melts against my parent's collective memory like a snowflake in summer. It is unfathomable to them that any parent would allow a student to get off as easily as Jonas does. What is life without honors classes?

You see what I have to live with.

"You could help him," my mother puts in, clearly uncomfortable with the notion of someone being satisfied with steady B's in a regular-track class. Maybe she thinks slackerdom is contagious.

Wait—maybe it *is.*

Nah, no way—if I were a slacker, I wouldn't have a Plan. Slackers don't plan, and certainly not in capital letters.

I look up, realize they're waiting on me for a reply. Right.

"You know," I say, noncommittal, "Jonas doesn't need help." At least, not in the ways that matter, the lucky bastard.

"Where's he going to school?" my father probes, leaning forward in his seat. His shirtsleeves swing dangerously close to broccoliville. He means college. That is, if kids who get B's actually go to college.

"Uh, well... the thing is, we're still only juniors." I can't believe I have to point this out. Again.

In other words: you're the only freaks who think my early admissions application to Brandeis should already be signed, sealed, delivered. This part I keep to myself.

"It's never too early to be thinking about college," my mother insists. She flashes a quick grin at Ben, who returns the smile angelically. It's entirely possible that he has a rough draft of his personal essay sketched out and saved in a desk drawer somewhere. And that he's had it there for a few years now.

You *see* what I have to live with?

In about four-point-seven seconds I am going to implode. I will have a comprehensive breakdown of the physical and mental variety. Total systems overload. My internal organs will boil over and dribble inward in violent protest of every single aspect of this meal. This conversation. This existence.

Not good.

"You're... right," I say, bobbing my head slowly. I can tell I've taken them by surprise. Awesome. I have a flash of what could be described as pure genius, if it weren't such a blatant rehash of our typical conversational loop. "That's why—that's why I'm going to go do some practice tests. Is that okay? Can I be excused?" I'm already pushing back from the table, palming my plate to load it into the dishwasher on my way upstairs.

"Sure, hon," my mother calls after me. "I bought you some new software. It should be in the plastic bag on your bed."

"Uh-huh." I take the stairs two at a time.

One of the good things about crazy overly involved parents? A shiny new MacBook waiting for me when I got home from Camp Ramah this summer. I didn't even have to ask.

What they don't know is that I can download from iTunes while I claim to be working. And I plan to keep it that way. They probably wouldn't approve of all the music that my counselor, Seth Rothstein, introduced me to over the summer. For instance, Lou Reed and the Velvet Underground. Lou Reed was the original hipster. Except even more hardcore, because he was completely sincere.

Also? He's Jewish. But that's neither here nor there.

Anyway, as for the parents and my musical proclivities, the thing is, I'm evolving. Mostly on the inside, yeah. For now.

The Plan is to move that evolution outward. The parents would not approve.

But, I figure, what *they* don't know can't hurt *me,* right?

• • •

Back in my bedroom, I stare straight ahead, in theory thinking about analogies ("TACITURN is to RETICENT as HOMOGENEOUS is to __________").

Thanks to my parents and their deep love of flash cards, I know what *taciturn* means. But unfortunately, I am not particularly focused on cracking this riddle amidst the small sea of multiple choices that swim before me on the computer screen.

Rather, what I am interested in—or, okay, if I'm going to be honest with myself, it's more like *fixated,* what I am *fixated on*—is the fact that Sari Horowitz has just logged on to IM.

To be precise, she logged on to IM four minutes and three seconds ago.

In the four minutes and three seconds that Sari Horowitz has been online, she has not IM'd me.

I am sorry to say that this is not, in fact, exceptional behavior for Sari Horowitz.

No, the likelihood is that Sari has logged on and been instantly bombarded with aggressively cheery Internet shorthand from alpha types. Jonas types, if not Jonas himself. Or else she was chatting with any number of the thirty or so close, personal girlfriends with whom she surrounds herself on a day-to-day basis. Or another guy, of course. Most likely her ex, Greg Schusterman. Greg is the bane of my existence. TACITURN is to RETICENT as BANE is to COMPLETE PEST. Greg is one of the only guys in our class who is as outright adored as Jonas is, if in a jockier, more mainstream way. So yeah, there's even odds that Sari and Greg are BFF online as well as in person. But that's a possibility I will myself not to entertain.

I debate IMing Sari, starting up the dialogue myself.

Hey, I could say. *What's up?*

It's short. Peppy. To the point.

It's lame. It couldn't possibly compete with the barrage of IMs a girl of Sari's social caliber receives.

Yo, what up?

No way. I don't have the street cred.

Hi.

Bo-ring.

And anyway, it's only been—I check the clock on the upper right-hand corner of my computer screen—four minutes and fifty-eight seconds that she's been online, now.

I mean, I can't, like, *jump* all over her. That would just be weird.

If Brandeis—or rather, how to break my lack of interest in Brandeis to my parents—was foremost on my mind this summer, then Sari Horowitz (as in, the relative attractiveness of/best possible ways to alert her to my availability as a romantic partner) was, if not totally equal, then a very close second.

Let's just say that Sari occupies a decent amount of my mental space.

I sigh. This is hopeless. There was a girl—her name was

Leah—over the summer, who had a crush on me. I only know this because her friend, a tiny, cherubic girl called Beth, cornered me outside of the mess hall and told me so. Leah was totally cute: petite, curly black hair, freckles. But she wasn't Sari. And unfortunately for the Leahs of the world (or, I guess, for the Leahs of Camp Ramah at least), when it comes to unrequited obsessions, I've never been much for the multitasking. I'm all Sari, all the time.

I'm also pathetic. Not only that, but I'm really just pissing away prime analogy-finding moments. I am acutely aware of the fact that my parents are all-too-onto me, to the precise moment since I tipped my chair back and cleared my plate from the dinner table and promised to them that I was going upstairs to take a practice SAT. I have at least forty minutes until they start knocking, showering me with well-meaning but high-pressure questions about scoring percentiles. When that moment comes, they are definitely going to expect that I have completed the test.

Or, at least, the analogies.

Breathe, I remind myself. *Homogeneous.*

There's a quiet, almost imperceptible knock at my door. My heart does a rail slide. It couldn't be my parents. I still have *at least* thirty-seven minutes before I'm supposed to be finished with the test.

The door opens before I can reply, which is how I know that it's Ben. He positions himself in the doorway dramatically, drawing himself up to his full four feet and three inches. He has a smudge on one cheek that I truly hope is a popsicle smear. His hair is unbrushed and hangs in unruly thickets over his forehead. He has managed to achieve maximum dishevelment in the fifteen minutes or so since dinner ended. Astonishing. Youth.

"What?" I ask as pissily as possible, deliberately turning back to the computer screen.

"Your music is *way* too loud," he brats. "I can't play computers."

Remember the thing about Ben being a certified geek? Yeah, that was no joke. At eleven, his two favorite pastimes are homework and "playing computers." He particularly adores being assigned extra credit projects. I mean, bizarre, right? Sometimes I worry about the kid, what with him being a socially maladjusted weirdo.

This is not one of those times.

"Blow me," I say, still fixated on my own computer screen.

"*And* you're not supposed to say curse words to me," he adds.

"*Blow me* is not a curse, freak," I say. "And I'm not turning the music down, so deal."

"It's just noise. It sucks," he says.

I resist the urge to inform him that (a) "sucks" is really just a variation on "blow me" and that (b) the Pixies is not noise. I mean, I just can't be bothered.

I'm momentarily distracted by the little *bloop-bloop* noise that means that I've just received an IM. There's a moment of anxiety as I wait for the window to fully reveal itself. And it's—

I recoil, startled.

SARILICIOUS42: U THERE?

Oh God, oh God, it's Sari. Sari just IM'd me.

SARI JUST IM'D ME.

Stay calm.

WRITE HER BACK!

The concepts of staying calm and writing her back are in direct opposition to each other.

I'm dizzy. Worse—I'm *reticent.* I think I might pass out.

Breathe.

I position my hands over the keyboard.

ILIKELOUREED: WHAT'S UP?

SARILICIOUS42: HOW BORING WAS ELKIN IN CALCULUS TODAY?

I have no idea. I spent the better part of Calculus contemplating the back of Sari's head.

ILIKELOUREED: RIGHT?

"Hel-*lo*!" It's Ben, aggressively apprising me of his continued presence in my doorway. "Are you on IM?" He somehow manages to make this sound like a threat.

"Ugh, *what?*" I ask, finally turning away.

"Why are you like that?" he asks, studying my exasperated face.

"Like what?" I *so* do not have time for this. The IM window flashes.

> SARILICIOUS42: THAT CLASS TOTALLY PUTS ME 2 SLEEP. ☺ TOO BAD, SINCE I'M TOTALLY, LIKE, FAILING.

"Like, all sweaty," Ben continues.

"I'm not," I huff.

"Yes, you are," Ben insists. "Why—are you talking to your *girlfriend*?" He pauses, contemplating the delicate nature of the boy-girl relationship. "I'll tell Mom you're not doing your SAT stuff."

Now he marches into my room, fully intending to stalk my IM conversation. Nu-uh. No. Unacceptable.

What's more, Sari's message is still open, and she's waiting for me to blow her away with some well-crafted witticism.

This is way too much pressure.

"Sa-ri-li-cious," Ben reads choppily, pronouncing every syllable. His eyes widen and I can see that he is mentally cataloging the girls in my class whose names he knows. Thankfully, there aren't many of them—one of the many benefits of Ben still being in middle school. He's at Gittleman, too, but it's a totally different campus.

(The various campuses of Leo R. Gittleman Jewish Day School are slowly—but comprehensively—taking over the greater Tri-State area. It's not even funny.)

"Okay, that's it," I say. I push back from my chair, nearly taking off Ben's foot in the process. "You're out of here."

"No." He plants his feet firmly.

"Yes." I think fast. "I'll tell Mom that you're disturbing me."

"I'll tell Mom you're not studying." He smirks.

Right.

Screw bargaining.

"Uh-uh," I decide, grabbing him by the shoulders and running him back out of the room as if he were a lawnmower. "*Later.*"

The hope is that by later on, he'll have forgotten all about this exchange. Though I admit that doesn't seem likely. For now, however, the crucial point is to respond to Sari before she loses interest in our non-witty non-banter.

That class totally puts me 2 sleep.

I'm toying with two different answers—one, enthusiastic and supportive: *I know!*; and one studiously casual: *ha ha.*

The first problem with both of these responses is that they are really only varying degrees of pathetic, thinly veiled grasps at a connection to Gittleman's "It Girl."

The second problem with these replies is that it took me about thirteen seconds too long to think them up. The tinny, electronic version of a door slam sounds from my computer, and with a sinking heart, I glance at the screen.

Yup. *Sarilicious42* is gone from IM.

TACITURN is to RETICENT as HOMOGENEOUS is to THE SAME OLD CRAP.

For now.

Sari wasn't wrong about Elkin's class. On a scale of one-to-boring, it rates about a sixty-seven, which by my estimations is somewhat on par with Saturday morning synagogue services. In other words, it's dull on a level that I actually find physically painful.

Usually I endure the excruciating forty-three minutes by staring intensely at the back of Sari's head, piecing together in my imagination either the front half of her outfit that day, or the conversation that I wish we would have after class ends. It's generally of the "Hey—call me later, Ari!" and "Sure thing, Sari!" variety.

We've been in school—in class together, in point of fact—for about a month now, and that conversation, humble though it is, has never actually taken place. But with all of the daydreaming that I do in this class, I will totally be ready for our exchange when the time is right. I could even provide Sari with notes for her lines. I mean, if she were so inclined.

Today, however, marks a watershed moment in my educational career at Gittleman. I'd be lying if I were to say that I'd gone the entire class period without once giving thought to Sari. But for the first time in as long as I can remember, our relationship (in as much as we are both carbon-based organisms comprised of eighty percent water) is not the A-plot in my head right now.

No, today my thoughts have turned to yet another semi-impossible task (one that would only seem less-than-daunting when compared to my absurd fantasies about taking Sari as my date to the annual Gittleman Purim Prom). I've managed to get to the point where I can eke out a reasonably-euphonic tune on my own guitar, so now it's officially time to put the Plan in action.

And this afternoon, I have a goal.

I need to convince Jonas that he can play bass.

I have no compelling reason to think that Jonas *should* be able to play bass. The presence of an upright piano in his family room leads me to suspect that at one point or another he took lessons. Probably he could plunk out an earnest, if bare-bones, rendition of "Heart and Soul" on request. But if Jonas ever took piano lessons, they marked the beginning and the end of his musical career—save for his recent forays into air guitar. And we all know how I feel about his singing.

It simply will not do.

Never mind that Jonas has never expressed even a modicum of interest in bass or, for that matter, any music not found on the Top 40 charts. I need him to expand his stylistic horizons, to think outside of his woefully under-catalogued iPod. I need Jonas to listen to me. Because I have a Plan. A Plan that will take us places. Lou Reed places. *Sari Horowitz* places. If we're lucky.

Of course, I am somewhat aware—in some far-flung nether-region of my dusty brain—that for himself, Jonas doesn't really need my Plan as much as I do. I want to be going places; Jonas is already there. Jonas is the type of guy that Sari makes it a point to say hi to, before *and* after every class. So I have a lot more riding on Jonas' potential interest in bass than he does.

I just hope I can get him to see it my way.

The bell rings, snapping me out of my trance. Jonas wastes no time in pushing back from his desk and stowing his notebook under one arm. Jonas never carries a book bag; that would be way too plebe. It confounds me, even as I stagger under the weight of my own backpack.

It must be noted, however, that Jonas is also often found without the right book in a given class. I suppose that for people like Jonas, this doesn't matter the way that it might to me. He's not daunted by the occasional detention. Whereas, my parents see detention as the first step on that slippery slope toward a lifetime of alcoholism, unemployment, and possibly various other unnamed, depraved perversions.

No, it doesn't make sense to me, either.

"Ari, man, I'll see you after math," Jonas calls. We're in separate math classes. Somehow I managed to place in the advanced track. Suffice it to say that Jonas did not. Yet another aspect of his high school career that does not seem to affect his emotional well-being. Whereas, when I informed my parents that I was going to be taking Calculus II, their reaction was so extreme, so unexpectedly, disproportionately excited, that I wondered for a moment if they had perhaps misunderstood me. They're very into "MATH!"

"No, wait up," I shout.

He lopes easily toward the doorway, the casual walk of the unselfconscious. I, on the other hand, am all angles and edges as I struggle to get to him before he disappears down the hall and is swallowed into the swell of faceless ponytails and bobbing, multi-colored yarmulkes: the entire Gittleman student body changing classes in one synchronized mass.

"What's up?" he asks, confused, as I clap one hand on his shoulder.

I take deep, gulping breaths, trying to calm my heartbeat before he notices that I am wheezing for air. It might be time for me to take up a sport of some kind. Gittleman doesn't have a football team—somehow, it's just not a very Jewish game—but obviously Jonas plays basketball. Point guard. Sari is the team manager, which, near as I can tell, has something to do with collecting the orange cones before and after practice drills and otherwise interacting with the players. Greg Schusterman was one of last season's starters.

If only I weren't too short for basketball.

"I wanted to talk to you."

He raises his eyebrows. "So, talk. But hurry up, man. I have Lipschitz next and she's going to f^&*ing kill me if I'm late."

No, she's not. Miss Lipschitz is about twenty-three years old and has as much control over her classroom as a hand puppet. She also has a markedly unsubtle crush on Jonas, which is one part gross, three parts hot. I mean, Miss Lipschitz is cute, as far as teachers go. "Are you busy after school?"

He frowns for a moment, concentrating. "I don't think so. You wanna hang out?" He breaks into a grin. "You want me to kick your ass at Mario Kart?"

"Yeah, that'd be cool," I say. Not. "But I actually just wanted to talk. About a plan. I mean, something I've been thinking about."

I'm not making any sense.

"You're not f^&*ing making any sense."

"I know. But trust me. I've got an idea for us."

Jonas rolls his eyes. "Spit it out already, man."

I sigh. "*Whatever.* We'll talk later. We can go to my house."

"Are your parents going to be home?"

"No. Dad's working late and Mom's got a Hadassah meeting." My mother is a big supporter of charitable causes. Give her a tzedakkah box and a cordless phone and she's probably only about three hours away from raising the equivalent of the GNP of a small independent island.

"Kosher," Jonas says. "Later, then." He taps at my closed fist with his own. Something else that he picked up at Camp Habonim. It's not much of a secret handshake if you aren't discrete about when and where you use it, of course, but I resist the urge to share this thought with Jonas.

"Kosher," I repeat.

I am sort of repulsed by myself as I say it. But hey—if you can't beat them, join them.

• • •

"Dude, man—what the f^&* is that?"

"Fender Telecaster," I say, lovingly fondling the scratched black enamel of my brand-new previously-owned electric guitar.

Jonas raises an eyebrow. "Where did *you* get the money for a guitar?"

"Camp Ramah," I remind him. I've been a camper there for ages now, and was a CIT (and sometime–Seth Rothstein groupie) this summer. Not what you would call a high-paying gig, and of course my parents insisted that the paycheck go directly toward my Brandeis fund (they call it a "college fund," but their thought process is as transparent as the Lucite mezuzah they've hung in my bedroom doorway). Still, I managed to pocket a small stash of tips that was mine, all mine. And in the meantime, to rip all of Seth's playlists.

"I thought Telecasters were f^&*ing expensive."

This is a surprise to me. Not that Fenders are expensive, because, I mean—duh. Rather, I did not realize that Jonas' knowledge of anything musical extended beyond his misplaced obsession with Adam Levine and that weirdo from Counting Crows with the messed-up hair. (What is it with musicians, by the way? Am I going to have to eventually screw up my own hair? 'Cause that could be... an improvement, maybe, now that I think about it.)

"They are. But I scored this one off of Craigslist." Hence the initials L.M. etched into its surface with what looks like the edge of a paperclip, and—heresy—a *Family Guy* decal stuck, indelibly, smack to the left of the strings. I mean, I enjoy *Family Guy* as much as the next intensely bored, unmotivated couch-surfer might, but the sticker doesn't exactly scream "rock 'n' roll" to me.

Whatever. I guess a secondhand guitar is going to have to be sufficiently rock 'n' roll for the foreseeable future.

"F^&*, man." Which is Jonas' way of telling me that he thinks the guitar is cool.

"Hey—" he continues, straightening up in his seat like an exclamation point. He's been hunched over my desk banging away at my computer ham-fistedly, prior to his momentary Fender-based distraction. Now he's at full attention, which I think is unrelated to the guitar. "Man, did I show you the last email I got from Larafromcamp?"

He did. At least three times. He showed me the attached JPEG as well. He calls it up again now, on the monitor, for good measure. Awesomely, an image of hot Larafromcamp and her hot sister on vacation in hot Israel. A perfect trifecta of heat.

My mistake was in bringing up Ramah. If I'd wanted to sustain Jonas' attention, I should have been more vague about the fundraising involved in procuring the guitar. I am painfully familiar with the fact that Jonas will twist any reference to summer camp into an excuse to name-drop his own sexy Jewess girlfriend, Larafromcamp. They met at Camp Habonim this past summer. To hear Jonas tell it, it was lust at first sight, and it's all been very hot and heavy ever since.

If Larafromcamp has her own last name, it's long been discarded, if not completely forgotten, by Jonas.

Larafromcamp grins at me from a glittering Tel Aviv beach. She looks great—hot, as usual—but I can't let myself get sucked in. I have to steer Jonas back to the original point of the conversation.

"Dude, the guitar."

"Right," he says absently, still staring at the computer screen.

I step forward and click swiftly but surely. Lara's enormous, exceptionally white smile fades to a tiny pinpoint before completely disappearing.

"What the f^&*, man?" Jonas' eyebrows come together in a show of extreme displeasure. Lara-ogling is one of his most beloved pastimes, all the sweeter if he can moon over her picture in the presence of a love-starved friend.

"I want to start a band."

This is it: the reason I asked Jonas over to my house, the reason I spent all of my camp cash on a secondhand Fender. My big Plan for junior year, my scheme for getting noticed—and possibly getting Sari at the same time.

Jonas blinks. "Can you even play?"

In response, I drag my amp—also secondhand—out of the deepest corners of my closet. I plug the guitar in and turn the amp down to its lowest setting (no eleven for us). Mom and Dad are out and Ben has some tutoring session, but I still live in fear of being outed. Playing guitar—playing *rock* guitar—is definitely not on the approved list of Brandeis-focused extracurricular activities. I strum the first few bars of Nirvana's "Lithium," knowing as I do that Kurt Cobain will have maximum impact on Jonas. Sucker has no idea that the man knew, like, three chords.

Jonas' eyes widen, impressed, and I know that I've made the right call.

"Dude, you can f^&*ing *play*," he comments when I've finished.

I don't bother to point out that a monkey could play "Lithium." For right now, I need Jonas drinking the Kool-

Aid. Otherwise he might not want to get involved. And I've been thinking.

"You should be bass."

Jonas looks startled. "F^&*, you think?"

I nod. "Totally. You'd be awesome at it. And it's easy to learn."

This is not, strictly speaking, true. But where Jonas is concerned, flattery is the surest path toward winning him over.

Jonas shakes his head back and forth a bit as he mulls. I can tell he's warming to the idea, already envisioning himself onstage, surrounded by swooning fans of the female persuasion.

"Your parents would kill you," he points out.

"Yes. That's why I've planned out an aggressive campaign of not telling them." Easier said than done, sure, but I'm willing to put in the effort. I'm no stranger to creative thinking when it comes to my parents and their multitiered rules and regulations.

"That could work." He purses his lips together. "I could sing."

I try not to flinch. We're all fully familiar with my assessment of Jonas' skills as a crooner.

"I'd f^&*ing rock out as lead singer."

I'm still not convinced.

"I'm not doing it if I can't be lead singer."

Then again, I personally can barely carry a tune. And if anyone has the potential to carry a band on charm alone, it's

Jonas. So yeah, he can be lead vocals. The whole "screeching, painful, animalistic wailing" thing can be our signature sound.

Talk about punk rock.

"We need a drummer," I say. "For sure."

"And a chick to bang a tambourine," Jonas adds. I wonder furtively if this is some sort of complicated euphemism, and then decide that I'm giving Jonas too much credit.

"Tambourine girl is negotiable," I say, not wanting to piss him off too early in our start-up. "Drummer is not."

"Fair enough," he agrees. "Who did you have in mind?"

I take a deep breath. "Yossi Gluck."

Jonas' eyebrows shoot toward his carefully-tousled hairline. "Are you f^&*ing serious?"

I nod grimly. "Serious as Yom Kippur, man," I assure him.

"Why? Why Yossi f^&*ing Gluck?"

"One reason. His parents wanted him to learn to play klezmer or something. Over the summer, I mean." I've looked into this, confirmed all of the rumors.

"What the f^&* do I care about that? Klezmer? So he's got lousy taste in music."

"You're missing the point," I say. "He's got *drums*."

THE FEIN RESIDENCE...
POLLOCK AT THE WHITNEY
HEY MOM, I NEED A BASS GUITAR. PREFERABLY A FENDER PRECISION, PREFERABLY IN BLACK, PREFERABLY WITH A MARSHALL STACK AMP.
WHY DO YOU NEED A GUITAR, HONEY?
MEMOIRS OF A GIRL WITH A GOLD NECKLACE

UH I'M STUDYING THE EFFECTS OF LOW FREQUENCY VIBRATIONS ON THE GROWTH OF A RARE SPECIES OF CENTRAL AMERICAN FLORA FOR THE SCIENCE FAIR.
LEFT BRAIN: WOW, WHERE DID THAT COME FROM?! RIGHT BRAIN: I KNOW, SWEET, RIGHT? LEFT BRAIN: HI FIVE!!!
I THOUGHT THE SCIENCE FAIR ONLY WENT UP UNTIL THE THIRD GRADE
YEAH, THEY CHANGED, THAT.
LEFT BRAIN: NICE SAVE. RIGHT BRAIN: THANKS BRO.

YOU KNOW, IF YOU'RE REALLY INTERESTED IN FLORA YOUR UNCLE CARL KNOWS A BOTONIST WHO..
WHAT MOM? I CAN'T HEAR YOU! YOU'RE BREAKING UP! BAD SIGNAL! TALK LATER!
LEFT BRAIN: DUDE I THINK THAT TACTIC ONLY WORKS WHEN YOU'RE ON A CELL PHONE. RIGHT BRAIN: LAST I CHECKED I WAS CREATIVE DIRECTOR AROUND HERE
THE WHITNEY

three

I shouldn't have mentioned Yom Kippur. Really, Passover would have been the better, more apt analogy.

See, the thing is, for better or for worse, among the general population of Gittleman High School, the name Yossi Gluck is most commonly associated with chocolate-covered matzoh. Never mind that matzoh of any sort is generally reserved for those seven torturous days in spring when we commemorate our forefathers' exodus from Egypt; never mind that chocolate-covered matzoh, especially the *dark* chocolate variety, bears a close resemblance in both taste and texture to tree bark. Yossi Gluck—and, in fact, *all* of the extended Gluck family—equals Passover. Matzoh, macaroons . . . the whole damn seder plate.

Stay with me.

"You're out of your f^&*ing mind, man," Jonas says, shaking his head in amazement at how completely and fully I appear to have gone off the deep end. "You're nuts."

Our debate about Yossi Gluck, i.e., the relative punk-rockness of, has raged on well into the next day's lunch period. We're staked out in the library three tables away from where Yossi reads, mesmerized as usual by a dead language.

"I hear what you're saying," I tell Jonas, waving my hand at him in a "let's all be reasonable" sort of gesture.

And I do. Hear what he's saying, that is. His concerns are not unfounded, after all. Yossi's yarmulke, required headgear for all Gittleman males, is perched askew atop his head and he chews absentmindedly on the cap of his pen. It must be preferable

NAME: YOSSI CHAIM GLUCK
DATE OF BIRTH: JULY 2ND 1993
HEIGHT: 5'-6"
ACTIVITIES: STUDY OF RABBINICAL INTERPRETATIONS OF SCRIPTURE
INTERESTS: HALACHA
KNOWN TO SAY: "THE TENSION BETWEEN MAN'S RATIONAL NATURE AND HIS CONSTANT SEARCH FOR SPIRITUAL FULFILLMENT IS NOWHERE BETTER ILLUSTRATED THAN IN THE WRITINGS OF THE RAMBAM."

to the untouched, unleavened, out-of-season snack food that sits just to his right (food of any sort is technically prohibited in the library, but I guess that special privileges are granted to the most righteous).

Even from where we sit, I can see a thin strand of drool slowly making its way down Yossi's chin. The effect is not very punk rock at all. What's my angle going to be?

Then I see it. The angle; the hook, line, and sinker. I jab Jonas in the rib. "Look."

He follows my gaze to underneath Yossi's table, where we can see his knee bobbing up and down in time to a rhythm only Yossi can hear.

Jonas cocks an eyebrow at me. "F^&* that, man. That means nothing. I mean, maybe he's got Tourette's or something."

"Can't you tell? It means he can keep time. If he can keep time with his knee, imagine how he'll rock out when he's sitting behind a sweet drum set."

It's a stretch, but I'm desperate. No one else at Gittleman has drums (have I mentioned it's a small school?), and we *have* to start a band. My Plan is taking on shades of obsession. It's not pretty. Any minute now, I'm going to start sweating the way I do when Greg Schusterman is in charge of picking dodgeball teams in gym class. Ugly stuff.

"He's going to crush our coolness quotient," Jonas says, leading me to speculate briefly on just how and when he learned the word *quotient.* But I can't be distracted from my mission.

"You're wrong," I insist, knowing as I say it that Jonas hates to be corrected. I've got to close this. It's time for my ace in the hole. "He's the key. He's so earnest it's ironic. And what's cooler than that?"

Jonas nods thoughtfully but says nothing. Still, I can see he's considering it. Which is something. Jonas loves unintended irony. For the hipness *quotient.*

"Think of Napoleon Dynamite," I implore. "Like, if he were Jewish."

"Larafromcamp loves that movie," Jonas says, a goofy smile breaking out over his face.

Everyone loves that movie. "Well, I mean . . . talk about rock 'n' roll."

The glint in Jonas' eyes means he's warming to my scheme. I've found my in.

"Think of him as . . . the Jewish day school answer to David Byrne," I suggest.

It's an inspired tactic. Jonas doesn't know who David Byrne is, really, but he knows that he *should* know. He knows that it's cool to know about David Byrne in a non-Gittleman, non-Abercrombie, non-Short Hills Mall sort of way. So rather than expose his ignorance, he's going to cave.

Jonas bites his lip and sighs. "F^&* yeah, man," he exhales. "Maybe you're right. I mean—yeah. You're totally f^&*ing right."

I resist the urge to high five myself. That would really ruin this moment. And this moment is one that I'm going to want to savor for a good, long while. In my mind I pick Jonas up and twirl him around in an impromptu dance of joy, but hastily set him back down again, mentally, when I realize that technically this is a little bit creepy.

Of course, we've still got one more hurdle to get past. We've got to somehow convince Yossi Gluck, dedicated Jewish scholar and full-time mensch, that he is completely and totally—to borrow Jonas' words—"rock and f^&*ing roll."

I'm thinking it's going to be easier said than done. Yossi could care less about cool, after all, as he has so thoroughly demonstrated on more than one occasion. But we've got a secret weapon: no one, to date, has proven impervious to Jonas Fein's smile.

Mensch or otherwise.

• • •

The thing about Gittleman is that contrary to popular belief, it is not a strict yeshiva. It's actually a "religious day school founded on the tenets of the varied and liberal traditions of the Conservative Jewish movement."

At least, that's what it says on our official school website.

All that really means is that we have a pretty diverse student body. Not to sound like a recruitment brochure, but kids here come from very different families. I guess the majority of us come from true Conservative households; like, we go to synagogue on the high holy days, we were bar or bat mitzvahed, and we maybe keep kosher, at least inside the house. Obviously religion is sort of important to our families, or we wouldn't be at Gittleman, where Torah reading is held promptly at 10:17 every Monday and Thursday morning, and lunch in the cafeteria is BYO dairy-only. We go to Jewish sleep-away camps, where we meet Jewish girlfriends and boyfriends, and a good portion of our organized "fun" is centered around Jewish-themed activities (hence my long-standing dream of escorting Sari Horowitz to the annual Gittleman Purim Prom sometime between now and when we would be, potentially, neighbors in the Daughters of Miriam Jewish retirement community of West Orange, New Jersey).

In short, it doesn't bother me that my parents are semi-religious. While my bar mitzvah was not exactly a low-pressure affair, I wouldn't say I minded being the center of attention for an afternoon. I don't know that I would go so far as to say that it was the first time I felt like "a man in the eyes of the Jewish community," but I did feel special. Like I had maybe accomplished something. Which wasn't really such a bad feeling.

So that's me, Jonas, and about roughly sixty-four percent of the Gittleman student body: religious enough to find ourselves in a school where learning Hebrew, Torah, and Rabbinics is valued as much as learning English, history, and math—but not, you know, *hard core* about it.

Then there's the other thirty-six percent.

A smattering of these kids are fully secular, which stuns

me to no end. I guess their parents figure that this way, even if they aren't going to practice at home, they're giving their kids a foundation in Jewish learning. And Gittleman is known for its academics, too. But myself, I think I'd be bummed if I had to go from eating cheeseburgers at home to conjugating Biblical Hebrew at school. That double-life thing has to be a killer.

But what do I know?

Anyway, the remainder of the thirty-six percent are what my mother likes to call (truth be told, rather sniffily), "High Conservative." These kids come from families where keeping kosher means only eating in Rabbi-supervised restaurants, and Shabbos means no electricity, no driving, *nada.* Dating outside of the faith is strictly *verboten*, though in all likelihood the possibility would really never be entertained.

Yossi Gluck, of the Short Hills Glucks, falls firmly into this, the latter category.

Yossi was born into a Northern-Jersey legacy, an influential family that had made its fortune in a certain brand of kosher-for-Passover condiments. The library at Gittleman was donated by, and therefore named after, the Glucks, as were various wings of nearby synagogues and JCCs. Yossi's family is large, and most of his first cousins attend a proper yeshiva over in Rockland County, New York—the kind of place where girls have to wear skirts to their ankles every day. No one is quite sure why Yossi and his younger sister Reena, a freshman, are here at Gittleman, but I suspect it has something to do with a shorter commute (from the little that I know of her, Yossi's mom seems to be the type to dig on convenience).

This means that Yossi is, almost by default, one of the most religious kids in the junior class. He is also slightly, um, socially challenged, and thus, as discussed, spends his lunch periods in his namesake library, poring over texts so ancient I'm not sure what language they're written in. I suppose I could ask, but if and when one ever manages to rouse Yossi from his books, the expression one is met with is one of such extreme confusion, mixed with terror, that to disturb him seems just plain cruel.

You might be surprised that any of us would actually concern ourselves with someone so deeply enmeshed in the social fringes of our little school community, but the truth is that Yossi fascinates us all. Honestly, we don't have much other excitement going on day-to-day. There are only sixty juniors, after all, and there are also only so many fables circulating about Larafromcamp. So at a certain point, we sort of have to make our own fun.

Yossi and I have Creative Writing together. He sits behind me and has gotten no higher than a C on any of the homework we've handed in since school started. I know this for a fact because Mrs. Fogel, a Gittleman mainstay who's taught me going on three years now, told me as much in a desperate and perhaps mildly inappropriate plea to get me to work with Yossi and bring his homework grades up.

Unfortunately, Yossi doesn't want my help. He is fine

with C grades, as are his parents. They must not be especially worried about his chances of getting into college, which makes a little more sense when you think about their ability to pave the way for him via a new Gluck Hillel center, or a Gluck kosher cafeteria. Not that I'm bitter. It isn't that I wish my parents had more money. I mean, we're fine, and I have my Craigslist guitar, after all. It's just that the idea of parents laying off once in a while sounds seriously blissful.

Still, if there's truth to the gossip mill, Yossi's parents are not only hands-off, they're also incredibly encouraging of the slightest sign of life. They must worry about his terminal weirdness almost as much as I do. Yossi's father is very active in the temple community, and supposedly he has high hopes for Yossi to follow in his footsteps. Yossi's mother, though, is somewhat less pious.

Now, admittedly, my familiarity with her is limited to a few awkward encounters at science fairs, but I've still managed to form an opinion. My take? She practices orthodoxy to appease Yossi's father, but as a general rule, prefers to demonstrate affection and faith through the consumption and distribution of material goods. The best anecdote I'd heard about her was that she had happened to notice Yossi making good use of his chopsticks one night last year out at Chef Wong's, and decided, for his birthday, to buy him a drum set. Something about how he could pursue his "passion for the sounds of klezmer music."

This makes Yossi that much more intriguing to me. I

hadn't had occasion to contemplate his passions, after all, before now.

In fact, between my borderline obsession with Yossi and his bizarre contentment to live life beyond the pale of popularity, and the fact that he actually possesses a functional set of drums, he's basically a ringer as drummer in the new band. To me, the choice is obvious.

• • •

Yossi puts down his pen and scratches idly at his temple. It's our chance.

"Hey, Yossi," I say in a casual, amiable voice, sidling slowly over to his table. The last thing I want to do is sneak up on him. "What're you reading?"

My breezy tone has caught him off guard nonetheless. He looks up at me, panicked, and starts in his seat so wildly that he nearly sends his book flying off the wide expanse of polished oak tabletop. "Uh—"

"Maimonedes?" Jonas asks, incredulous. My spirits plummet, though I don't know what Yossi could have been reading that wouldn't have blown Jonas' mind. He's probably not big on *Men's Health* or *Maxim*, after all.

Yossi blinks furiously. The effect is not flattering. "It's a critical examination—"

"—*Cool*," I say, cutting him off with a level of feigned enthusiasm that makes me sound like a drugged-out Jehovah's Witness. It is imperative to my mission that Yossi's religious fervor be reined in, big-time. "Totally. So," I continue, slowly gaining my conversational bearings, "Jonas and I have been talking."

"About me?" *Blink, blink.* It's a twitchy-eyeball morse code.

"Sort of." I glance over at Jonas, who is gnawing on a hangnail intensely. This is not the level of attention that I might have hoped for. I need to step up the pace of my pitch. "See, we're starting a band."

"Oh?'

"Yeah. And I'm going to be lead guitar, and Jonas is going to be bass—"

"Who's going to sing?"

I experience a brief flicker of annoyance. Yossi isn't supposed to ask questions. Besides, everyone knows that you don't need to be able to sing in order to have a band. In fact, if you're off-tune, it's almost *more* punk rock, actually.

"Uh, we're going to sing," I say, flustered. "Both of us."

Yossi nods. "My sister sings in the school choir."

"Yeah," I say. Like, what does this have to do with anything? "So," I say, warming to the heart of my pitch, "we heard you have a drum set."

"Huh?" Yossi's forehead scrunches up in confusion. "Oh, yeah. My mom got it for my for my birthday"—this in a tone of voice that suggests that his reaction to the gift was less than enthusiastic—"to play klezmer, when I learn. We set it up in the racquetball court."

Okay, then. The racquetball court. Check.

How many jars of gefilte fish do you think one has to

sell in order to finance a racquetball court? Just out of curiosity.

Shut up, I tell my innermost, questioning mind. *Focus.*

"Sounds like it'd be a great place to practice," I offer. "Big, probably soundproof... away from the rest of the house."

"Yeah, I guess," Yossi says, thoroughly noncommittal.

Jonas pokes me in the ribs and I realize we've got about three and half minutes until the period ends.

I go for broke.

"We're looking for a drummer. What do you think?"

The blinking makes a valiant comeback, this time accompanied by a turbo-charged chewing of the lower lip. "You want me to be in your band?"

I shake my head in the affirmative. Jonas coughs.

Yossi shrugs. "I have ... " He gestures toward the enormous book in front of him wordlessly, as though the sheer weight of the burden of the Jewish scholarly tradition has rendered him speechless. "Reading."

"You have *drums*," I say, feeling slightly panicked. In another moment Jonas is going to bolt. Then we'll be left without drums *or* a potential drummer. And while I know that Jonas has a low-level, misplaced God complex, he certainly can't sing, play bass, *and* drum all at the same time. Just ... no.

"I think you'd be awesome. And"—okay, here goes nothing—"isn't it, like, a *mitzvah* to spread the word of God through music?"

Now I've got Yossi's attention. "It's going to be a Jewish rock band?"

I pause. There's really no way to tell Yossi what he wants to hear without outright lying. I look at Jonas. What I wouldn't give for one of his easy, bright, cure-all grins. But no, he's tapping his foot impatiently like he maybe has to go to the bathroom or something. And the bell is going to ring any second.

I clear my throat, stalling for time. Yossi blinks again. He really should think about getting that checked out.

Jonas hitches at his notebooks, resettling them in the crook of his left elbow, then lifts his free right arm and runs his fingers through his hair—carefully, so as not to accidentally neaten his purposefully tousled effect.

All at once, Yossi gasps and sits straight up in his seat. I spend a split second worrying that the blinking has progressed to a full-on brain embolism, but realize quickly that he's actually staring at Jonas' wrist.

"You guys are into kabbalah?"

"What?" Now *I* blink.

Yossi gestures toward Jonas' arm again.

Oh, right. The red string around Jonas' wrist. Larafromcamp sent it to him after she saw a picture of Lindsay Lohan wearing one on E! Online. He never takes it off and I have wondered on more than one occasion what it must smell like by now. It looks pretty grungy.

"Right, oh—totally," I say, recovering. "Jonas' girlfriend is a *big* follower." Of Lindsay Lohan, but why split hairs?

"Huh," Yossi says, and I can see that we've got him. Once again, Jonas and his all-consuming charm have come through for me.

Even against his own better judgment.

four

It feels like everything should be different now. I don't know how, exactly. Maybe, like, crackling sparks of divine energy should be shooting out from me in every direction. Something. I should be glowing with some kind of heavenly halo. An actual, literal aura of coolness. That is, if guys can have halos. Halos might be a chick thing.

Anyway. You get my point. I mean, I'm in a *band* now. So punk rock, right?

Unfortunately, nothing like this happens. I have no such halo, for better or for worse. In point of fact, my face is a little bit shiny, but I think that's more acne than anything else. Not quite the same thing.

The day after Jonas and I talked Yossi into joining our band, I woke up feeling like someone who recently discovered how to turn paper clips into gold bars, or how to absorb the contents of a three-hundred-page book simply through the powers of osmosis. But my surroundings reflected nothing of the awesome personal transformation to come. Absolutely nothing of any significance happened, other than my mother reminding me that she needed me to stay home with Ben after school that evening because she had "meetings." I was a little bit put out, sure, but not in much of a position to protest. The next night, Jonas had basketball practice. Putting sports before the band—not cool. I decided to say something about that at band practice, but realized that this would be difficult to do if the band didn't, uh, *practice.*

It was a conundrum. And my skin wasn't clearing up, either.

Now, almost a week later, I teeter valiantly between exploding with frustration or, alternately, melting into a molten puddle of anticlimax and disappointment right here on the second floor, outside of the Gittleman library. At least Ellie the librarian looks like the type who'd pitch in to wipe up after me when I'm gone.

My plastic super-shell is starting to soften and warp. It's a metaphor—duh—for how I'm so completely losing it. This won't work. Determined, I finally corner Jonas outside of his English class.

"Practice tonight?"

He looks surprised for a moment, but then bumps his fist toward mine in the unsecret handshake. "For sure, man. Totally." He makes rock 'n' roll horns with his hand and I flinch.

I can't believe that this guy is going to be responsible for my social salvation. He's making *devil horns.*

The universe is unjust and cruel.

Relief snakes its way through my bloodstream anyway. "I'll tell Yossi." That, I can definitely do—especially if it means Operation Make Me Cooler is a go.

• • •

When I do find Yossi to let him know, it's instantly clear that he was hoping we'd forgotten about our little pact to collectively subvert the suburban indie rock scene.

"Tonight should . . . work," he says cautiously. He doesn't blink, even though I can tell that he really, really wants to. Maybe he's working through this little physical tic, trying to conduct himself in a manner more befitting of a drummer demi-god. "I just have to call my mother."

I clap him on the shoulder. "Meet you in the parking lot after the last bell." Amazingly—and also, traitorously—my own hand wants to curl itself up into a facsimile of Jonas' devilish rock 'n' roll horns, but I make like Yossi triumphing over the blink and prevail through the sheer force of willpower. Gravity takes over and my hands do normal, handlike things, such as hanging straight down at my sides awkwardly.

He tilts his head quizzically. "I take the bus."

Of course he does. Like the blinking, this is a habit best broken early. "Jonas will give us a ride."

Obviously Jonas, blessed with both an early birthday and intensely permissive parents, has not only his driver's license but also a big, screeching gas-guzzler. Screw the environment, right?

But, I mean, I am in no position to proselytize. *I* have to screw the environment by proxy. I don't have either a license or wheels of my own yet.

The need for Operation Make Me Cooler is so completely dire, urgent, overwhelming.

And I can't believe I've rested its potential success on Jonas Fein and Yossi "Klezmer" Gluck.

• • •

I had no idea there was so much money to be made in kosher Passover condiments. But clearly it's a racket.

I mean, if Yossi's house is a reflection of his father's success, then apparently what the world needs now is matzo-meal and non-dairy "butter" spread—in bulk. You could fit at least three of my houses into his pool shed. His *pool shed* is bigger than my whole house. A lot bigger. It peeks out imperiously from behind a slatted wooden fence as Jonas pulls into the Glucks' driveway.

"Jeez." Jonas whistles approvingly as we make our way

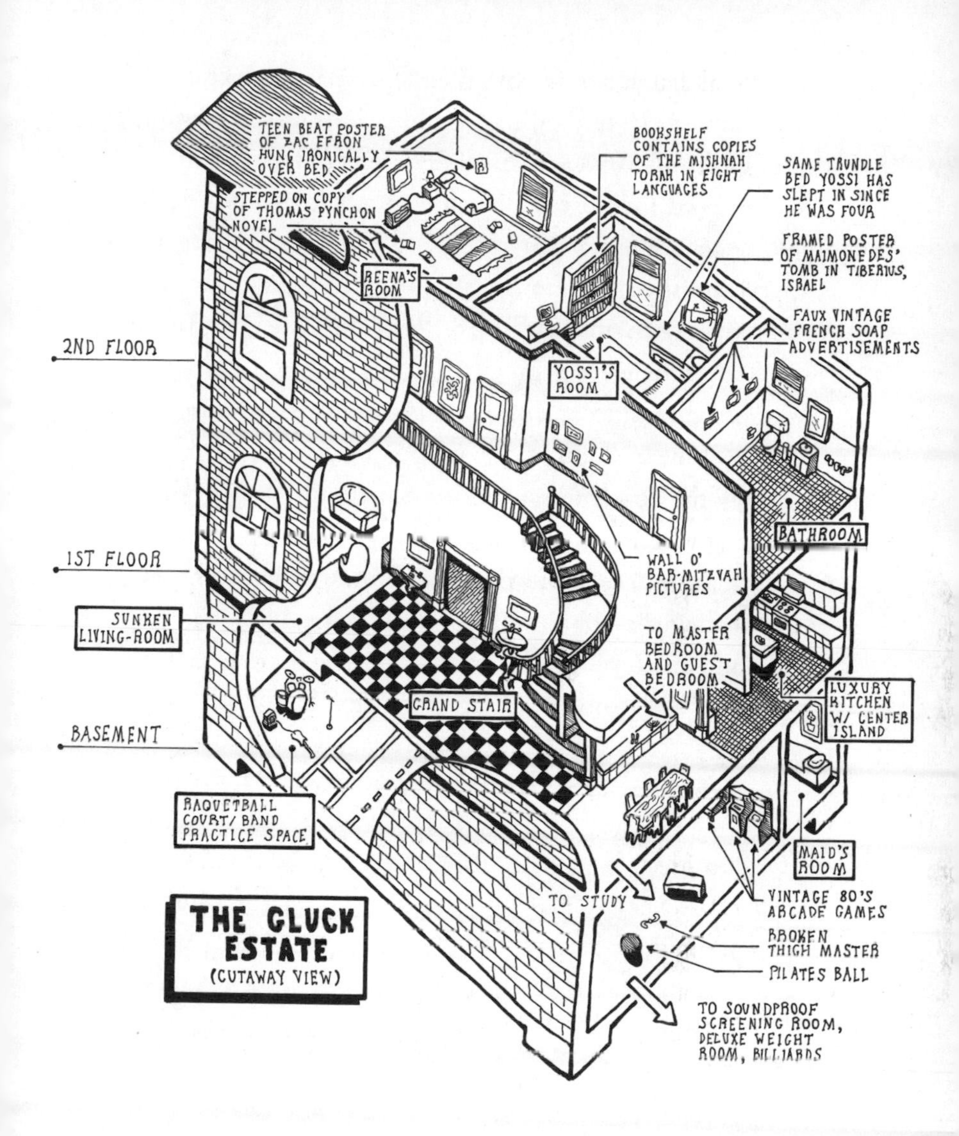
TEEN BEAT POSTER OF ZAC EFRON HUNG IRONICALLY OVER BED
STEPPED ON COPY OF THOMAS PYNCHON NOVEL
REENA'S ROOM
BOOKSHELF CONTAINS COPIES OF THE MISHNAH TORAH IN EIGHT LANGUAGES
SAME TRUNDLE BED YOSSI HAS SLEPT IN SINCE HE WAS FOUR
FRAMED POSTER OF MAIMONEDES' TOMB IN TIBERIUS, ISRAEL
FAUX VINTAGE FRENCH SOAP ADVERTISEMENTS
YOSSI'S ROOM
2ND FLOOR
BATHROOM
WALL O' BAR-MITZVAH PICTURES
1ST FLOOR
SUNKEN LIVING-ROOM
TO MASTER BEDROOM AND GUEST BEDROOM
LUXURY KITCHEN W/ CENTER ISLAND
GRAND STAIR
BASEMENT
RAQUETBALL COURT/ BAND PRACTICE SPACE
MAID'S ROOM
THE GLUCK ESTATE
(CUTAWAY VIEW)
TO STUDY
VINTAGE 80'S ARCADE GAMES
BROKEN THIGH MASTER
PILATES BALL
TO SOUNDPROOF SCREENING ROOM, DELUXE WEIGHT ROOM, BILLIARDS

inside—through the marble-tiled foyer, past the extremely huge, extremely sunken living room and into a yawning, gleaming, and unpleasantly chilly kitchen. I mean, there's just no need for the temperature to be set to *arctic*. Also, the room is lousy with reflective surfaces, making me appreciate my own mother's lowered interest in domestic trivialities. Seriously, you'd need sunglasses just to eat breakfast in here every morning.

Yossi dives into one of the upper cabinets and busts out a package of crackers (thankfully, leavened. I mean, in this house, I'm thinking you never know). He peers into the refrigerator. "We have ... juice ... and some diet soda."

Diet soda is repulsive. I honestly have no idea why girls drink it. Or why Yossi would, for that matter.

"Diet soda is repulsive."

Huh?

I double-check to make sure that I didn't actually say that out loud, and realize right away that I'm good. But still puzzled, because in walks Yossi's younger sister, Reena. She's a freshman. And also, apparently, clairvoyant.

She stretches her mouth into an exaggerated grimace in Yossi's direction. "Besides, Mom will *kill* you if you finish her Coke Zero." She shakes her head slowly. "She is Out. Of. Control."

I smile. I've hardly noticed Reena in school—she doesn't hang out with the high-profile girls in her class, the ones who are always somehow slathering their mouths with some kind of fancy lip balm, brushing their hair, and frantically text-messaging their twelve-hundred-and-three closest friends all at the same time—but maybe she's funny?

At least, I don't mind being kept in the loop as to where she stands on the matter of artificial sweeteners.

Reena pours herself a glass of water from the kitchen sink and settles comfortably at a stool by the center island. She's seated herself directly across from Jonas and me, and dumped a notebook, a paperback, and a mechanical pencil onto the surface in front of her. The book has seen better days, and it may be only slightly older than the bowling shirt she's wearing that says *Pam* over the pocket on its left breast.

Not that I'm looking at her left breast. Or the right one.

Jonas cocks his head to one side and pulls his patented fingers-through-the-hair move. He grins indulgently at Reena. "Might not get a lot of reading done in here," he smarms. "It's, you know, the first official meeting of our band. Our *rock* band." And then the horns again. I didn't know Jonas could smile that wildly, and frankly, I think I preferred the bliss of ignorance.

"Our *garage*-rock band. *Indie* band," I put in. It's a notable distinction, even if said distinction presently eludes our hapless frontman.

Reena nods her head slowly, managing not to look too freaked out by the charm that slowly oozes from Jonas' pores, or by my own music-geek spazz attack, either. "Right. Yossi told me." She presses her palms against the island and I see that though her nails are bitten to the quick, they are also painted silver.

Yossi told her? On some level, this is good news. At least it means he wasn't completely trying to repress our conversation from the other day. He acknowledges that he is in a band. This is an important first step.

She quickly twists her hair up and off of her face. "So, I mean, are we going to have, like, a set practice time from now on? 'Cause I think that would be a good idea. To get into a rhythm, you know?"

Again: huh? What's all this "we" business? The last thing we need is some kind of low-grade Yoko getting in the way of our superstar ascent.

I look at Jonas. Maybe he was serious about wanting a girl and a tambourine and stuff. "Did—" *Did you know about this?*

I can't. There's no way to end that sentence politely, not with Reena sitting right there across the table from me. Yoko or not, I really don't have anything against her.

"That's the thing," Yossi offers. His neck turns a blotchy shade of pink. It's not a good look for him. "I meant to tell you guys. My parents—"

"They don't want us practicing here?" I knew it was too good to be true.

"They're fine with us practicing here," he assures me, "as long as it's not on Shabbos."

"Check. We are shomer Shabbos, one and all." I can do that. Heck, I'll blow the shofar for the Glucks at the next Rosh Hashana synagogue service, if it means we can practice in their racquetball court.

"But they—"

"They *insist* that I be in the band, too." Reena makes the Coke Zero face again. "Because I'm not, uh, *social* enough for their liking." I take this to mean that, as previously noted, she is not the fancy lip balm, text-messaging type. "If Yossi is going to be 'branching out'"—she actually curves her fingers into air quotes, looking pained—"then I have to branch out, too." She shudders and rubs the back of her neck with her hand. Her silver fingernails glitter against her hair, which is black to the extreme.

Jonas leans forward so that his elbows rest on the island. "Do you have a tambourine?" His eyebrows raise into twin arches. I groan.

Reena groans, too. Could it be? Is there a female to be found on the whole of the East Coast who can withstand the charisma of Jonas Fein? Amazing. *Almost* amazing enough to make up for the fact that she seems to want us even less than we want her.

I hope she knows that she has to buy her own tambourine.

She folds her arms across her chest. "I sing."

She sings?

"She sings," Yossi confirms, his throat returning to a normal hue. "She, uh ... she was in the Gittleman Middle School Hanukkah choir!"

Right.

"Because it's a mitzvah to spread the word of God through music," Reena says, looking directly at me.

So that's it, then. Reena is a faithful, choral, foot soldier of Hashem, and she won't be denied. And now, we've got—oh, no—our Yoko.

Otherwise known as Pam.

• • •

Exactly twenty-six minutes after our first band practice has begun, Jonas announces that he needs to "bail." He's got a phone date with Larafromcamp. I am distressed but try to play it off, suggesting that we meet regularly every Tuesday right after school. Everyone agrees, and I can't help but notice that I'm the only one who's really excited about this. I mean, Jonas is into it, but he's not, you know, freaking out or anything.

I guess that's a good thing. Freaking out is really not very punk rock.

I give out an assignment: "We need to come up with a band name."

Yossi looks dubious. Reena looks bored. Jonas looks appalled at the idea that we've got band homework.

"We need to learn how to *play instruments*," Reena offers as an alternate opinion.

Jonas' cell phone chirps insistently. He fishes it out of his messenger bag and flips it open. "Yo." He wrinkles his forehead in an approximation of deep concentration, then grins. "Yeah, you know…" He tilts his head back toward the rest of us, nods, and then turns back away from us again. "I'm gonna have to call you when I get home. Should be twenty minutes." He clicks the phone shut again and turns to me. "Ready, man?"

I nod, grabbing my own stuff. "Remember about the name," I say. Names are so important. Like, the Velvet Underground by any other name would *not* sound as broody and thoughtful and indie and stuff. I'm a little worried about the name thing.

Jonas grins. "F^&* that. We can call ourselves the Jonases!"

You see why I'm concerned.

"Just kidding, man," he laughs, hooking his thumbs into the front pockets of his jeans. I know him too well, though—he's only maybe seventy-three percent kidding. If I had gone along with him, we would definitely be debuting as the Jonases.

"Everybody think," I say, following Jonas out the front door.

Please.

• • •

I see names everywhere I look. In my bedroom: *Universal Remote, Broken Alarm Clock, The Erasable Pens.* On the way to school: *The Blue Hydrants, Narrow Shoulder, Neighborhood Watch.* At the mall: *The Double-Tall Espressos, Acupuncture for Pets, White Sale.*

My names suck (except for "Acupuncture for Pets"; I may be onto something there). It's a pretty bad sign: if I'm not even cool enough to name my band, how can I possibly be cool enough to be in the band, in the first place?

"What's 'No Turn on Red'?"

I snap to attention to see Ben pointing. I bought a notebook over the weekend, for writing songs and stuff. I think that's what musicians do. Especially the deep ones. Kurt Cobain even published a whole book—like his journals or something, with artwork, and lyrics, and essays and stuff—and that was after he died. I don't plan to write any essays. And I don't think I'd want anyone pawing through my notebook without asking, even if I were dead. But still, it seemed like a solid investment. *College Ruled.*

"What's 'College Ruled'? Why do you have such a weird list in there?"

I grab at the notebook, close it, and pull it to my chest protectively. "It's not weird. I mean, it's nothing."

A typical morning...
(And Band Names Originating Therefrom)
-FLYING TOAST-
ixnay
Some recurring dreams were best left unspoken of. Still, what the hell could it mean?
ARI, WAKE UP AND TAKE YOUR RIGHTFUL PLACE AS KING OF TOAST-LAND!
GO AWAY! I KNOW NOTHING OF TOAST-LAND!
-DENIAL
-DENIAL!
-DENIAL?
HEY ARI, WHAT ARE YOU DRAWING? IS IT DIRTY? MOM, ARI'S DRAWING DIRTY PICTURES.
-THE MINOR IRRITANTS
-I wish one of his friends would tell him that ThunderCats shirt is not cool.
-SANKA
-SANKA!
-DAD'S SHAVING MISHAP
-THE MINIVANS
OW!
YIELD
Add handle, resembles dustbuster
GOOD BOY.
NOVA
-LEASHWALKER
Leash (no dog)
-SQUIRRELS IN LOVE
-Uh, don't really know how to draw this one.

He's not buying it. "It's something."

Yeah—and it's something my parents can't find out about. Not even if we named ourselves *Twenty-Four Hundred, Advanced Placement,* or *Early Decision.*

"Forget about the notebook." I prod him. "Finish your math and we'll get pizza." Bribes are always a swift failsafe, especially those revolving around melted cheese and tomato sauce.

Ben nods. "Kosher." He scratches his pencil across his math workbook with a shade more focus than a moment ago.

"We don't—" I begin to remind him that we aren't that religious. We can't have pepperoni or sausage on our pizza, but beyond that it's all good. But then I realize: he means "kosher" like "cool," the way Jonas uses it. He must have heard Jonas say it sometime recently. The long arm of Jonas' cool-quotient has finally stretched down the hallways of Gittleman, all the way to the lower school campus. It has embedded itself in my brother's brain. Ugh.

Still, I could kiss him. My brother, I mean, not Jonas. And even though I *could* kiss him, I don't. My mind is already revving up, charging down my mental expressway. I can't believe I have to wait until Tuesday. I *can't* wait until Tuesday.

Now, I have an idea. And it's so, totally, *kosher.*

five

Today, Reena's fingernails are purple. And her expression is completely blank. She yawns, covering her mouth with her hand.

"Band names?" she asks, with absolutely no inflection at all.

"Did you come up with any?" On the one hand, I'll be kind of pissed if no one has any names, because, you know, that's what we were supposed to do. But on the other hand, if no one has any names, we can just go with my brilliant brainchild. It might be a win-win kind of deal.

"The Wind-Up Birds," she volunteers. I deflate slightly, having no idea what she's talking about.

"Uh, no," Jonas says. "That doesn't even make any f^&*ing sense."

She sighs. "It's the name of a book." She slaps at the ever-present book in her lap for good measure. "*God.*"

"Rock stars don't read." Jonas winks at Reena, totally not getting the fact that he's basically just repulsed her. There is one female specimen in this universe, at least, who is repulsed by Jonas.

It's kind of cool. Even if she does have lousy taste in band names. Lou Reed probably read books and all, but we need something with a little more punch.

I peel back the cover of my notebook. I sort of don't want the rest of them to know about the notebook, or to see all of the stuff I've been writing in it, so I aim for nonchalant. The good news is that no one's paying any attention to me, so the nonchalant thing is a huge success.

Yossi, Reena, and I are collapsed in respective heaps against the far right corner of the Gluck racquetball court. As predicted, Jonas' parents were more than happy to buy him a top-of-the-line Fender Precision, which currently rests up against my own guitar, free of secondhand stickers and showing my sorry instrument up. Unsurprising. Unlike the rest of us slumped on the floor, Jonas is seated at Yossi's drum set, fooling around with the drumsticks, distracted.

I clear my throat. I'm still in nonchalant mode, so it's

distressing that the sound is something like a chain saw starting up. Jonas even looks up from the drums.

"I had an idea." Like it just came to me right this second, hand-delivered by the ghost of Jim Morrison. Like I haven't been rehearsing my delivery since I had my flash of divine inspiration last week with Ben. "Um, what if we called ourselves, you know, Kosher Boys?"

There is a deathly silence during which I imagine not having ventured the statement. Ahh, bliss.

"Well, for one, I'm not a boy," Reena points out.

Huh. Somehow I'd managed to block out that small detail. But still. We aren't wind-up birds, either, are we? I regroup, go the conciliatory route. "Right. Okay, well, just Kosher, then."

The silence reverberating in the room makes my ears ring.

After a painful seventeen—no, nineteen—seconds, Yossi speaks up. "I don't get it." He really looks like he doesn't, either. The blinking is back.

I sigh. "It's ironic, you know. Like, when Jonas says, 'kosher.'"

I forget that, until the formation of our nameless band, Yossi and Jonas didn't talk to each other all that much. News of this addition to the Jewish American slang lexicon may not have made it to Yossi just yet.

"Ironic." Reena looks pensive. I have no idea how she feels about irony. I mean, clearly she's a literary type, but still.

"But..." Yossi bites his lip and blinks again. "I *am* kosher."

I shake my head. "Not the point, dude." Did Yo La Tengo have this much trouble getting themselves off the ground? I look to Jonas for backup, but he is gnawing away at a fingernail.

"I know!" he says, pointing an index finger into the air with a burst of energy. "The Tribe."

I roll my eyes, waiting for Yossi's inevitable—

"I don't get it."

Jonas leans forward excitedly. "Like, because Jews are, you know, 'members of the tribe.'"

"They—"

"They are," Reena cuts in, nodding at Yossi affirmatively. He snaps his mouth shut.

"But . . ." *But what about* my *brainchild? What about* my *genius? What about "Kosher Boys (and Girl)"?*

"If we're going to call ourselves something, you know, jokey and abstract like 'the Tribe,' why not just stick with 'Kosher?'" I ask, my voice a notch higher on the pitch scale than I would like. Nonchalant. Not.

Jonas sticks out his tongue in his best Gene Simmons impression. It's the oral equivalent of devil horns. "Because," he says, grabbing at the drumsticks and busting out a slow, Specials-style rhythm.

Because. Of course. Because when Jonas is in the room, he's the leader of whatever is going on in that room. It's why I wanted him in the band, in the first place. It's the reason that he's playing bass.

Wait, though. That beat he's hammering out right

now—my head's nodding in tempo like it's got a life of its own.

I'm not the only one whose head is bobbing up and down. Yossi is mesmerized, his gaze fixed on a point just in front of the drums, like he is meditating on the out-of-bounds zone of the racquetball court floor.

"I like that," he says, and even though he's half-mumbling when he says it, it's clear that he means Jonas' drumbeat.

Jonas sticks his tongue out again. "Duh." *Tappity-tap-tap.*

"I, um, didn't know you listened to klezmer." Yossi's face is doing the splotchy thing again.

Now Jonas sits up straight in his seat, clutching the drumsticks in one hand. "Klezmer?" He shakes his head no. "Nu-uh. That's a ska beat, man."

The thing is, they're both right. I never realized how similar klezmer and ska were before. But this rhythm could totally go either way.

Yossi and Jonas may each have a different membership, but they're both card-carrying members of the tribe.

And, I guess, members of the Tribe, too.

For what that's worth.

• • •

Gittleman High loves itself a good assembly.

This Wednesday, the theme is: "Zionism and You: Gittleman for Peace in Jerusalem NOW!"

I am all for peace in Jerusalem (seriously; you can't

spend so many years in this cult compound without getting at least semibrainwashed, and really, who is actually *against* peace, when all is said and done?). Unfortunately, though, these assemblies are generally little more than a flimsy excuse for Principal Friedel to show us slides from her last summer vacation to the Holy Land. We file into the auditorium during third period (and may I add that I am not at all sorry to be missing Calculus this morning?), and settle ourselves into hard plastic chairs, at once enveloped in a familiar cocoon of static electricity.

"*Boker tov,* students," Friedel begins, craning her head to see out over the podium. The Jews are not a tall people. "Good morning. We have a real treat for you today!"

Unlikely.

I say as much to Jonas, who sits at my left wrapped in quiet concentration, deftly texting Larafromcamp. He's completely off the teachers' radar, somehow. He really can be so smooth sometimes. That, or the teachers are way too into our special "treat" to assert any real authority.

Friedel clears her throat. "As you may know, the Gittleman Upper School Choir—"

—we have an upper school choir?

"—has been practicing for Israeli Appreciation Day—"

—we have an Israeli Appreciation Day?

"—and today we're going to get to hear them practice for the big event!"

She steps back from the podium to tepid applause.

It's hard to get very worked up over a group I didn't know existed, and a holiday I'm 99 percent certain is made up.

One by one, the members of the Gittleman Upper School Choir shuffle onstage. They resemble nothing so much as anemic zombies (with marginally better hair). I toy with the zipper on my backpack, itching to fish out my notebook and zone, when I realize something and sit up with a start.

Reena's onstage. In the choir. She's in the second row, third from the left, and Ally Leirhoff's explosive Jew-fro threatens to devour her face whole, but she's for sure there. And she actually looks ... happy. Like, not exceptionally cheesed-out to be participating in something wholly unironic like the Gittleman Choir.

Odd. I highly doubt the wind-up bird would approve.

Then again, there's precedence for this. She did sing in middle school. Almost proudly, I've heard.

Our music teacher and *de facto* choir leader, Ms. Weiner (and yes, it's pronounced exactly like you hope it is) lowers herself dramatically onto her piano bench and launches valiantly into a medley of contemporary Jewish songs. Her entire body shakes as she plunks down on the keys. She is clearly fully enveloped in the mitzvah of song.

It's the standard Gittleman hit parade: "Jerusalem of Gold," "Jerusalem is Mine," and, just for kicks, "Land of Milk and Honey." The arrangement sways in and out of Hebrew, lulling me likewise in and out of consciousness, until Reena perkily pulls herself out of the double-rowed crescent of singers, gliding forward until she's standing alone at the side of the stage.

Never before have I heard "Erev Shel Shoshanim" rendered with such soul. The song is about an "evening of lilies" (huh?), but the way Reena sings it, it could be the latest single from Norah Jones. This is make-out music territory we're veering into. And the sultry vibrato of her voice isn't the least bit diminished by the denim skirt/white tee shirt uniform dictated for all choir performances (blue and white being the national colors of the Holy Land, of course).

The girl can *sing.*

The tiny hairs on my forearms prickle and stand at attention. I had no idea that the combination of a basic Gap tee and Israeli folk music could be so hot. But it is. It's hot on an unfathomable level. It's, like, Larafromcamp hot.

I glance around the room. Poker faces, and some kids are for sure flat-out sleeping with their eyes open. If anyone else's arm hairs have gone stiff, they're not showing. But I don't care. She's good, it's obvious. Better than good. She's *amazing.*

This is huge. In a flash, Reena's gone from being our Yoko to being our Nico. She's Kim Deal mixed with Ani DiFranco (the early years), with a dash of Regina Spektor sprinkled in for good measure. Guys are going to lust after her the same way that girls go nuts over Jonas.

We're going to have guy fans!

This could easily double our fan base.

Like, just the fact that we may even *develop* a fan base (excluding Jonas' ego, that is) is enormous.

I elbow Jonas in the ribs. "Check it out."

He pockets his phone. "Huh?"

"Reena."

Jonas glances at the stage. "She's wearing black checkered Vans." It's clear from his tone that this is not a good thing. I think someone told him that Chuck Taylors were the only way to go, and he took it to heart. Poor Jonas.

I take a chance. "I know. Old-school, right?"

"Right!" He covers well. Even Jonas understands the implication that vintage equals instant cool-cred.

"I didn't realize she had a good voice," I continue.

"She's in the choir," Jonas points out, reasonably.

"Lots of people are in the choir," I remind him. I mean, there are, like, twenty-five curly-haired zombies onstage singing backup to Reena's big-finish finale right now. None of them look very pleased about it, but still. There they are. "She's the best one."

How did she manage to hide the fact of her major skill from us last night? Oh, right—we spent the whole practice watching Yossi and Jonas do a call-and-response ska/klezmer showcase, then argued for a little bit about whether or not to invest in band uniforms (outcome: negative. We couldn't agree on appropriate indie-wear, and we weren't going to be caught dead wearing the Jewish-star tee shirts Yossi had seen on ChosenCouture.com).

There is one way, I realize, to help Jonas embrace the magnitude of this moment. "This is awesome," I say, trying to sound literally awe-struck. "You guys are going to *rock out* together."

Jonas squints for a moment, no doubt envisioning their mutual rockage. After a beat, he nods, and I know that as always, appealing to his ego has proved an efficient mode of persuasion.

"We're gonna have to rethink our set list," he offers finally, "and come up with some duets. To showcase us together." He grins.

"Set list?" We have no set list. We don't even have a list of three songs that all four of us can play.

Come to think of it, we don't even have a list of three songs that all four of us can *name.*

"For the gig."

Now I am really confused. Unfortunately, the choir presentation is winding down, and so is the last reserve of Friedel's patience, as she has at some point during the performance woven herself into the aisle. She taps me on the shoulder and makes a violent *shhhshing* gesture when she finally manages to catch my eye.

I'm risking detention, but I've gotta do it. Because I think I heard Jonas say,

"A gig? Like, with us playing music?"

Out loud? In front of other people? Um, when?

"Yeah, man. I lined it up." He winks. "Who's your lead guitarist?" He says it in a "who's your daddy?" kind of tone, which is really sort of gross.

And besides—*I* am, technically. *I* am lead guitarist. "You're bassist."

"I am the *smoothest* bassist this school has ever seen!"

He whispers so fervently that he showers me with a light spray of spittle. Smooth.

He leans back in his chair, undaunted by the laws of science as pertaining to static electricity and Semitic hair, and clasps his hands together behind his head. "We are going to f^&*ing rock, man. I can't wait."

I can.

If I were really punk rock, I guess, this would be good news. However, as it is, this information is merely terrifying. Agh.

Yeah, I can definitely wait.

• • •

Sari corners me on our way into Elkin's class. Her hair is up in a pink plaid headband that's kind of dumb, but she totally rocks it, of course. She's with Melissa Mendel, her number-one sidekick (quick SAT analogy: MELISSA is to SARI as ARI is to JONAS). Sari's eyes are wide.

"Jonas IM'd me last night," she says, giggling.

Of course he did. Larafromcamp alone isn't enough for someone of Jonas' social standing. He won't achieve full Jonas-dom until such a time as every single female specimen at Gittleman has him programmed into their cell-phone speed dial (and that includes the teachers, too). And frankly, I think he's at least 88 percent there. That he has been IMing Sari supports my theory.

"Yeah," I say, unsure of how exactly one should respond to this non-information. I try to look like the thought of her and Jonas tearing up the keyboards strikes me squarely on the center of my inner happy-chord. But it doesn't. Although she's talking to me voluntarily, so I suppose I have him to thank for something, at least.

"He says you guys are in a *band*!"

What did I tell you? A band is like currency. The Plan is already wielding its magic touch.

"It's true." I shrug, all fake-modest.

She squeals. "That's *so cool*!"

Melissa bobs her head in a tepid demonstration of agreement. She looks like she maybe thinks it's lukewarm rather than cool per se, but I'm undaunted.

"Yeah, it was my idea," I say.

Sari shakes her head like it's all too much for her. "It's so cool," she repeats, her headband swaying back and forth in approval. Blurry pink plaid everywhere. Dangerous stuff. "You *have* to tell us when you're going to play."

I do, don't I? I mean, it's important to keep the fans happy, right? They're the ones who *really* make it all happen. Thank goodness for Jonas' shortsighted overconfidence.

"Actually," I say, still trying to play it like I couldn't care less, "we've got a gig coming up."

Or, you know—so I hear.

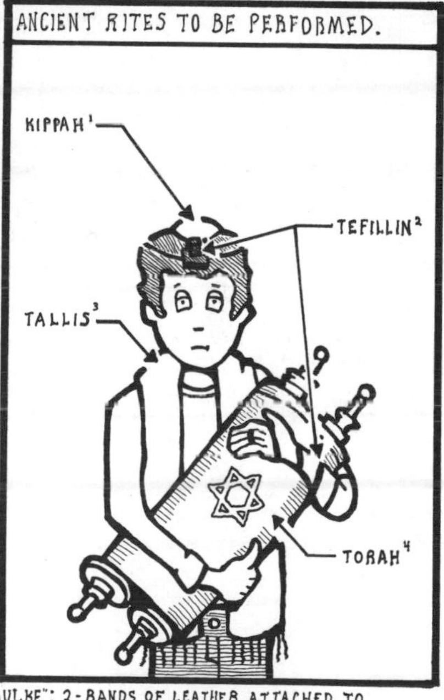

1- KNOWN POPULARLY AMONG NON-JEWS AS THE "YARMULKE"; 2- BANDS OF LEATHER ATTACHED TO BOXES MADE OF STIFF ANIMAL HIDE CONTAINING PORTIONS OF SCRIPTURE HAND-WRITTEN ON

IT MEANS THAT BLACK & WHITE ISSUES EASILY TURN GREY...

PARCHMENT. DURING PRAYER ALL MALE WORSHIPERS ARE REQUIRED TO AFFIX THIS ASSEMBLAGE TO THEIR HEADS AND LEFT ARMS BY MEANS OF A PROCEDURE PRESCRIBED LONG AGO BY THE RABBIS

OF YORE. I COULD TRY TO EXPLAIN BUT YOU'D DO JUST AS WELL TO HIT UP WIKIPEDIA; 3- TRADITIONAL PRAYER SHAWL. YEAH, AS IF THE MULTIPLE LAYERS OF ANIMAL HIDE

WEREN'T ENOUGH, THERE'S A SHAWL; 4- THE FIVE BOOKS OF MOSES AS DICTATED TO MOSES BY GOD ON MOUNT SINAI. CHRISTIANS SEE THE TORAH AS A KIND OF "PART 1" OF THE BIBLE,

PART 2 CONSISTING OF THE GOSPELS THAT DESCRIBE THE TEACHINGS OF JESUS. US JEWS PREFER PART 1 MAINLY BECAUSE GOD IS A BADA**. IN PART 2 HE HAS A KID AND KINDA GOES SOFT.

SIX

This one goes out to Ross, my cousin and my main man—today you *are* a man, my man!"

From his perch onstage, Jonas somehow manages to do the Gene Simmons tongue, the devil horns, and his impromptu little toast all at once, balancing his bass against his hip all the while. It's a nifty trick, I admit to myself grudgingly.

The way I see it, it doesn't matter that Ross Fein is, as of this afternoon, a bar mitzvah and therefore, technically, a man in the eyes of the Jewish community. Dude needs to sprout at least another three inches of height and cultivate one or two hairs on his upper lip, minimum, before he will officially qualify for the testosterone league.

But.

Today, Saturday, October 17th, marks a momentous occasion, not just for Ross Fein, but for the Tribe as well. We are playing. Live. An actual, honest-to-godlessness gig.

True, it's a bar mitzvah. Jonas' cousin's bar mitzvah, to be precise. I mean, it's a far cry from Woodstock. Or Lollapalooza. Or even a set at the Stone Pony. Like, Africa far. But try telling that to my stomach, which is currently practicing its survival-scout knot-tying techniques.

I knew I should have passed on the buffet whitefish salad. Now, potato salad, macaroni salad, caesar salad—*those* are salads. Whitefish is more like a death wish. A *kosher* death wish.

I strum idly on my guitar strings, hoping that I look less like someone about to revisit his *kiddish* nosh in reverse and more like a confident musician about to set Congregation Emanuel on fire.

That is, if fire weren't prohibited on Shabbos.

The truth is that for the strictly observant, fire isn't the only thing prohibited on Shabbos. Electricity and any form of "work" are out, too. So it's a good thing that Congregation Emanuel goes heavy on the partying, light on the tradition. We're free to rock out, now that we've got all the various members of the Tribe on board.

It wasn't easy, I'll tell you that, getting everybody on

the same page. And it wasn't just Yossi, with his primeval fear of the wrath of Hashem and everything godly and good. When Jonas first broke the news about the gig, I was dubious, too.

I mean, *synagogue?* I've made a regular practice of avoiding synagogue for the last fifteen years of my life (back at age one, I didn't have a whole lot of say in the matter, of course). But as always, what Jonas wants, Jonas gets.

Jonas Fein can be very persuasive.

• • •

"So what's all this drama about a gig coming up?" Reena slid down in her seat, exhaling loudly. "Everybody else seems to have already heard something about this. Including"—she rolled her eyes heavily—"Sari Horowitz."

So Reena knew Sari? Or rather, she kept tabs on Sari to the extent that she'd gotten wind of the latest grist for Sari's gossip mill? Hmm. I made a mental note to file away this information for later. It had to be valuable, somehow. I wasn't totally sure how—girls are such a mystery—but still. Check. Information for later.

"Yeah." Jonas grinned. "Now we got a buzz going."

"Fair enough," Reena breezed. "Can you, um, maybe share the buzz? I, for one, would love to . . . buzz."

"It would be helpful if we could all buzz together," I agreed. Not to be a dick or anything, but really.

"This Saturday. My cousin's bar mitzvah."

It was on the tip of my tongue to ask Jonas what his

cousin's bar mitzvah had to do with our gig, when it dawned on me. Wait.

"Wait." Once again, Reena had managed to chime in with my thoughts before I was even aware of them. This was getting sort of spooky. "We're playing at the bar mitzvah?"

No way. This was problematic for various reasons, namely:

A bar mitzvah is the Jewish tradition of calling a boy or girl up to read the Torah at Saturday morning service when he or she reaches the age of thirteen. The term *bar mitzvah* literally means "commanded son," meaning that, with the opportunity to lead the community in a Torah reading, one has taken on all of the commandments implicit in Jewish adulthood. Fun times, right?

But actually, these days it is sort of fun, as mainstream conservative Judaism has warped and molded the typical bar mitzvah into a fete on par with something you'd see on MTV's *My Super Sweet Sixteen*. The year I turned thirteen I attended no fewer than five bar mitzvahs with Texas Hold'em as a theme. I have a desk drawer at home littered with custom-designed play money stamped with the names of various classmates and the respective dates of their receptions.

Jonas' cousin's bash promised to be one of the more lavish parties I'd been to in a while, but I still wasn't convinced it was the right time or place to debut my sweet licks. In addition to my general wariness re: religious ceremony, there was the pesky fact that we still couldn't play any one song from start to finish. And a typical bar mitzvah reception ran for four hours or so. Even if we did learn one song between now and the gig, one song sure as hell wasn't going to carry us for four solid hours.

"And you're not concerned about the fact that we really don't have a repertoire, as such, just yet?"

God bless that mind-reading Reena and her complete and total lack of filter.

"We've got time to practice," Jonas said.

I allowed myself a brief instant of relief. It was quickly shattered, however, when Jonas went on to add, "The bar mitzvah isn't until next Saturday."

"Next Saturday?" My voice rose to an embarrassed squeak.

"Relax," Jonas said, his voice calm and reassuring. It was the aural equivalent of Japanese garden, all crisply trimmed hedges and greenery, and it was beginning to work its Fein-mojo on me. After all, what was a band without a gig? Trumped-up karaoke night, that's what.

"We only need to learn one song," he explained. "They've got a band booked already, but they'll let us play one song. It's perfect."

Dubious as I was of the whole bar mitzvah scene—after all, I hadn't been doing a ton over the last few years to keep up my end of the bargain as a Man in the Eyes of the Jewish Community—I had to admit that one song really did sound doable. Even if we ended up choking out a punked-out rendition of "Night of the Lilies." I mean, at least we knew Reena could sing that song. We could talk her into going a cappella, if it came to that. Possibly.

Reena nodded, more to herself than to any of us. "One song. That's do-able."

"Night of the Lilies" was looking like less and less of a long shot.

"Yeah, but"—it was Yossi, complete with signature splotch and blink—"not on Shabbos."

"What do you mean?" Jonas asked. He looked truly confused.

"Technically, Saturday would be the most logical day for a bar mitzvah," I put in, trying to keep the sarcastic edge out of my voice. I wasn't aiming to be confrontational, but honestly.

The truth was, the longer we sat there, the more the idea grew on me. One song at a low-profile event like a bar mitzvah could be just the shot in the arm our unlikely band needed to take our sound to the next level. Or the first level. Either way. So where did Yossi get off, being such a buzzkill?

"I can't drive on Shabbos," Yossi pointed out.

Oh. Right.

I'm definitely going to hell. Whatever the Jewish version of hell is.

"But Emanuel is walking distance from here," Jonas argued.

It was a great point. It was well-thought out and conclusive. It was not remotely typical of Jonas' general thought process, and suggested that he was maybe warming to the whole rock-god thing, as I'd hoped he would.

"Boy makes a good point," Reena said, further endearing herself to me as a defender of all things indie. We were like matching mismatched socks—no one was going to fold us together, that was, but there was something comforting about knowing that if the two of us were going to be stranded in the socks-and-underwear drawer, well, then, at least we'd be stranded, lonely little stray socks, together.

It occurred to me that the mutual concepts of underwear and Reena were making me blush. Odd. My blushing patterns were typically relegated to Sari-related experiences.

Anyway.

"Doesn't matter," Yossi said, mashing his lips together tightly. "You can't play music on Shabbos."

"But you can sing," I insisted. I didn't care if I was going to Jewish hell, I had to face it: this weird, cult-like branch of Judaism to which Yossi ascribed was starting to become a major pain in the butt. Or, you know—sort of inconvenient. Which was annoying.

"But you can't play an instrument," Yossi repeated, sounding vaguely Stepfordian. (Stepfordowitzian? Never mind.) He crossed his arms over his chest, as though daring us. "You can't."

"Coke Zero break," Reena cut in, waving her hands, rising, and making toward the door. "Anyone want anything?"

Jonas and Yossi shouted out their orders, still glaring at each other. "I'll help you carry," I offered, jumping up to follow her. Anything to get out of that room. Even a space as big as an indoor racquetball court could get pretty stuffy with all of that wadded-up resentment polluting the air.

We wandered upstairs to the kitchen in relative silence. It was a blessed contrast to the debate raging in the practice room, but still, I had to break it. For me there's no such thing as a comfortable conversational lull.

"I, uh, thought you hate diet soda," I coughed.

"I do," Reena said simply. "I'm in a bad mood."

"Oh." I didn't have much of a response to that.

"Here's the thing," she said suddenly, wheeling around to face me. Her twin braids whipped against her cheeks. "I think a gig is a good idea."

"Agreed." It was the mismatched socks thing again. Though I didn't dare go to the mental-underwear-drawer place.

"I'll get Yossi to the bar mitzvah," she promised. "Don't worry. You just make sure Jonas is there, and we'll figure it out."

She sounded so sure of herself, I assumed she had to be on to something. So I just held the refrigerator door open and tried to figure her out while she went bobbing for NutraSweet.

"You're kind of… full of it, you know," I said, the sentiment bursting from nowhere. But there it was, and it was real. And despite the fact that suddenly my hands were quivering from this confrontational vibe, I knew without a doubt that I was right.

She banged the refrigerator door shut with her hip and fixed her eyes on me. They were like something out of Picasso's blue period—the color, not the shape, obviously. "Excuse me?"

"This whole 'cooler than thou' thing that you've got going on. It's bull." My voice quavered. I have always been a party line sort of guy. As opposed to, you know, a "rile girls up for no real reason" kind of guy. "You're as excited by the gig as any of us." How did I know that? But I did.

"I just said I thought it was a good idea," she reminded me, peevish. "I'm not exactly trying to hide anything."

"You told us your parents forced you to join the band."

"They did." She popped the top on her soda can and took a long sip. I hadn't known until now that it was possible to sip angrily. And how.

"I heard you sing at the Israeli Appreciation assembly."

She shrugged. "So did the whole school. Attendance was mandatory."

"You're a good singer," I said, even though it was an understatement. "And you love to sing."

Reena lowered her eyes. I could tell that I'd managed to create the slightest of hairline cracks in her exterior. Those Picasso eyes were suddenly flickering gray. "Yeah, and?"

I smiled to myself. Ruffling Reena, however slightly, felt like a small victory. One that I wanted to savor, at least for a beat or two. "You want it," I said at last, smirking. "You want the band. You want us."

She took a long, final gulp of her soda and slid the can against the sink where the recyclables were stacked. "Whatever," she said, shaking her head. "I don't want you."

"Whatever," I echoed. Who cared what Reena wanted, anyway?

Not me.

• • •

So, that was our last practice. And Reena had come through—sort of. That is, she got Yossi to the synagogue. Unfortunately, she'd had to use some low-level subterfuge in order to do so.

When the two of them arrived at the party, it quickly became clear that Yossi hadn't thought we'd be playing. This was readily apparent when he warily eyed the equipment set up at the head of the dance floor and muttered, "I thought we weren't going to be playing."

"It's *one song,* Yossi," Reena said desperately. "It'll be fun."

Jonas shot me a questioning look, clearly concerned that this gig wasn't going to go off.

Meanwhile, Yossi was shaking his head, either in disbelief or flat-out disgust. "Low, Reena. Really low."

She had the good grace to look slightly abashed, but quickly recovered, sidling up to one of the refreshment

tables and scooping up a kosher, chocolate-dipped sandwich cookie.

"*What* did you say to him?" I sidled up to her and spoke in my best stage whisper.

She shrugged, wiping the sheen of sweat off her forehead. "I told him I was reading Torah today and I wanted him to be there to hear it." She took a bite of her cookie, made a face, and swiftly deposited it into the nearest trash bin.

Egad. She was a master of deception. Surely she is going to Jewish hell, eventually. No wonder Yossi looked extra pissed.

No matter; I totally expected Yossi to cave; after all, there was historical precedence for caving. He hadn't even wanted to join the Tribe to begin with, and here he was, eagerly awaiting our very first official gig. Minus the "eagerly" part, that was.

There was also a dark moment where I actually feared that Yossi would spin on one well-polished dress shoe heel and march right out of the reception hall. Marching was perfectly kosher on Shabbos, after all, and he seemed pretty disgusted about having been lied to. Especially what with Reena having invoked the word of God in her web of deceit.

We were deep in the midst of a four-way staring contest that I suspected was just on the brink of getting ugly, when the music blaring in the background came to a sudden halt and the squeal of microphone feedback filled the air.

"Ladies and gentlemen, we're going to take a quick break, but don't worry, because this next act is guaranteed

to keep you shaking your bar mitzvah booties. Give it up for—heh—the Tribe!"

Someone (the real band's drummer, probably), erupted into a frilly drumroll. A few of the more Manischewitz-soaked guests even clapped. This was it. Our moment had come. It was officially time for our first gig. But we couldn't very well go on without a drummer (unless the real drummer wanted to sub in for Yossi, but he sounded kind of excited about the break his band had coming up, so I thought probably not).

What was Yossi going to do?

Reena bit her lip. She looked pretty torn, but anyone could see that she really wanted to perform. I couldn't blame her. It wasn't a huge step up from the Gittleman Hanukkah choir. But it was something.

Yossi obviously saw it, and it was something to him, too. Chalk it up to the protective older brother thing. He glared at Reena, and then took a moment to glare at Jonas and at me, in turn. Then he sighed, grabbed Reena's hand, and made his way toward the drum set holding court at the front of the room.

• • •

So here we now stand, having taken the stage at Ross' bar mitzvah, teetering nervously against our instruments, the whitefish salad I consumed taunting me vigorously. Jonas finishes his intro, and Reena steps forward toward her mic. I am surprised to see that she looks a touch nervous, though she swallows and covers heroically. She grabs the microphone out of its stand and quasi-whispers a countdown, "one, and a two, and a—"

All at once, Yossi explodes into a frenzy of rhythm and energy. It's amazing—what he lacks in finesse he makes up for in sheer willingness to dorkify himself. It's like I told Jonas way back when—the Napoleon Dynamite factor. It *works.* For his part, Jonas bears down on his bass. I strike a power chord. And we're off. It's "Hava Nagilah" like you've never heard it before, with a ska-klezmer remixed beat, soft Sundays-style vocals, and a Pixies riff or two thrown in for good measure. We have no idea what we're doing, really, but we're original.

And honestly? We're kind of awesome.

Mi-Face.com

EARN YOUR COLLEGE DEGREE IN 8 SECONDS!
CLICK ON THE DANCING PROFESSOR!!!

HOME SEARCH LOG OUT

THE TRIBE

"THIS AIN'T YOUR RABBI'S MUSIC."

- ADD TO FRIENDS
- SEND TRIBE A MESSAGE
- FLIRT WITH TRIBE
- REPORT TRIBE

THE TRIBE HAS 18 FRIENDS
[SEE ALL FRIENDS]

COMMENTS [SHOWING 1 OF 1]

DUDES, YOU *ROCKED OUT* THIS WEEKEND! YOU'RE TOTALLY PLAYING MY BAR MITZVAH TOO! -SOON2BAMAN

-ADD COMMENT

LOCATION: NORTH JERZ
RELIGION: JEW-ISH
ZODIAC SIGN: REALLY?
SCHOOL: LEO R. GITTLEMAN HIGH

INTERESTS:
SECONDHAND GUITARS, SAT PREP, MECHANICAL PENCILS, FAN-BASES, PLAYING GIGS, THE TALMUD, KABBALAH, SUGARED SODA, JAPANESE MAGICAL REALISTS, MARIO KART, HOT CHICKS FROM JEWISH CAMP, SNOW DAYS, THE GITTLEMAN HANNUKAH CHOIR, ROCKIN' OUT.

MUSIC:
PIXIES, THE VELVET UNDERGROUND, YO LA TENGO, THE SMITHS, THE CURE, TORI AMOS, ELVIS COSTELLO, NEKO CASE, MIDTOWN, RANCID, JOHN ZORN, THE KLEZMATICS, THE SPECIALS, THE MAGNETIC FIELDS, IMOGEN HEAP, MATES OF STATE, THE KIMBALLS, THE STOOGES, BUILT TO SPILL, THE WRENS, INTERPOL, JOY DIVISION, BENNY GOODMAN, CAT POWER, ETC, ETC, ETC

MOVIES:
THE TEN COMMANDMENTS, SUPERBAD, THIS IS SPINAL TAP, LIKE WATER FOR CHOCOLATE, TRUE ROMANCE, BOTTLE ROCKET, CLUELESS, FINDING NEMO

TELEVISION:
PBS, COMEDY CENTRAL, "SCRIPTED REALITY" (GUILTY PLEASURE), "IRON CHEF", "AMERICAN CHOPPER", "THE OFFICE", "THE SOPRANOS"

BOOKS:
"THE WIND-UP BIRD CHRONICLE", "A CLOCKWORK ORANGE", "THE BIBLE (VOLS. 1-5)", "HOW TO WIN FRIENDS AND INFLUENCE PEOPLE (PGS. 1-12)"

HEROES:
LOU REED, HARUKI MURAKAMI, MAIMONEDES, JONAS FEIN

seven

What the f^&* is *Forever*?" Jonas coughs into his fist.

Reena rolls her eyes. It's what she does. Especially when Jonas is freaking out. "Hello? My favorite book. Or, er, one of them." She shakes her head at Jonas in wonderment. "The book that taught me about the fragile flower that is my budding womanhood?"

"Gah." Jonas makes a face.

Reena sighs. "Ask Larafromcamp. I'm sure she's read it."

"*People*," I cut in. "Can we focus, please?" The MySpace page was my creation and I do want feedback—but preferably of the non-moronic variety. I mean, it's probably a little bit soon to bust out with our own website or anything like that, but MySpace? For music? It's a no-brainer.

Less brain-free is my attempt to please all four band members with one profile. *Forever* is just the latest in a litany of hotly contested references.

In the end we decide that Reena can keep her Judy Blume if Jonas can keep his Jimmy Eat World. Myself, I'm not too sure about either. But whatever. And Yossi's still not talking to us.

"Hey, man—the Bible, volumes one through five. Good stuff, right?" I prod him. You'd think he would be cheery and bright; we're tucked away at one of the library computers during Monday lunch period. Boy is in his element. But he remains stubbornly indifferent to my brainchild.

"He's not talking to us," Reena explains.

As discussed.

"Dude, you are *so* overreacting," Jonas ribs. Of course, for his part, Jonas is *so* not helping.

"I get it, I do," I say, swiveling my chair so that I'm pretty much up in Yossi's face. He blinks and looks away. "We blindsided you. It wasn't cool."

"But it was awesome," Reena chimes in, patting him on the shoulder. She beams.

I smile, too. It was awesome, wasn't it? Yeah, it was only one song, but it was bar mitzvah appropriate (which is a fine line to walk, if you can believe it), and we were tight. We actually sounded like we kind of knew what we were doing. Maybe we *did* kind of know what we were doing. And props to Reena for finding a way to get Yossi to the synagogue when he was so obviously anti the violation of his day of rest, the Holy Sabbath.

"It was totally awesome," I confirm. "Yossi, you *rocked.* And okay, so we shouldn't have pushed you into performing on Shabbos, but tell me it wasn't a mitzvah, the way you helped Ross kick it, bar mitzvah-boy style?"

Reena nods, warming to my angle. "It's true. Every single person there was sharing in his special day. *And* we turned a really traditional folk song into something ringtone worthy." In fact, it's the song that cues when you call up our MySpace profile. It echoes tinnily away as Reena speaks, perfectly underscoring her impassioned rhetoric. Did she learn public speaking from Judy Blume? Probably not.

"Ring tone!" Jonas smacks his palm against his forehead like he just realized he forgot to cash in a winning lottery ticket or something, and darts off.

Reena looks at me. I shrug. Who knows? "Maybe he was distracted by something shiny."

Reena laughs, a short, snorting sound that I find oddly adorable. It's this laughter, however, that seems to finally set Yossi off.

"I told you I was shomer Shabbos," he says, so quietly at first that I'm not sure he actually means to be speaking out loud. "I told you right from the start."

Ouch. I might have liked it better when he wasn't talking.

"I know," I say. "And I'm sorry. I've been ... a little pushy about the whole band thing." A little. "I just, I don't know, I really wanted to try something new this year. You know? Next year is all about college applications, and my parents are crazed about Brandeis, and I just thought it could be fun to do what I wanted to do. For once. For now. While I can."

Whoa.

It's the truth, which Yossi seems to sense. He softens.

"I understand, I guess," he offers, clearly reluctant. He sighs heavily. "But I'm not doing it again."

I shake my head enthusiastically. "Of course not. Absolutely. You have your integrity, and we're all over that."

Besides, here's hoping that our next gig is a little bit bigger than a local bar mitzvah, anyway.

He braces his hands against the sturdy tabletop. "Fine," he agrees, still sullen.

Thank goodness Yossi's principles are of the more soft-spoken variety. Our little reconciliation was easier-won than I anticipated. I have to admit, I was worried for a nanosecond or two there.

And frankly, I don't mind sullen. Sullen I'll take. Sullen means we can move past this mini-drama and continue our quest toward indie-chart domination.

Or at least a mention in the *Gittleman Star.*

• • •

After lunch, I decide to make a gesture of good faith and walk with Yossi to Creative Writing. I have an idea that as we make our way down the crowded hall, people are looking at us. Nothing too obvious, you know, but a sideways glance here or there, like they're trying *not* to seem like they're looking, trying to be completely blasé. I guess in that sense, paradoxically, it winds up being all kinds of obvious. I myself am no stranger, of course, to the complex art of playing it cool. You can't try too hard. And then, suddenly, you're trying too hard. It's a delicate balance.

"I have to get my notebook," Yossi says, coming to a halt in front of what must be his locker. He whirls the combination lock, rummages distractedly inside.

He's going to need more than a notebook to rescue his grade from the toilet, but I keep this thought to myself.

"Ari!"

Sari must have hit the Crest Whitestrips hard this weekend—as she hones in on me, her teeth are practically glittering. They're all I can see. For a moment I am mesmerized.

I catch myself. "Hey."

She fumbles with a locker door. Sari is locker-neighbors with Yossi? How did I not know this? I want to mentally slap myself for the infinite missed "chance" encounters I could have orchestrated.

But it doesn't pay to dwell on what might have been. The point is, Sari is here, now, in front of the locker that I now know to be hers. And her timing is perfect, now that Yossi and I have one fewer degree of separation between us.

She pulls a teeny-tiny brush out of her turquoise sequined bag and runs it through her hair until it gleams as brightly as her teeth. Everything about Sari sparkles today. It's blinding. She peers into a mirror she's hung on the inside of her locker door, does something almost imperceptible to her bangs. After a moment, she's satisfied, shutting her locker door and shaking her shiny, shiny hair across her shoulders. I'm heading into daydream territory—Venus De Milo had nothing on Sari Horowitz—when she turns to us again.

"I *heard* about your show!"

"Well, technically, it was just the one song," I say modestly. I'm not *feeling* very modest, but I want her to think of me as humbly adorable, if insincere.

"Jonas said he was going to make your song into a ringtone that we could download."

"Jonas also says dogs can't look up."

"What?"

I realize the *Shaun of the Dead* reference is probably lost on Sari and try to cover my tracks. Where was I?

Ah, yes. Ringtones.

Jonas said he was going to create one? I think back to his sudden departure from the library. Now it all makes sense.

"Anyway," she goes on, "I can't wait to hear it."

"We'll play for you. You know—a private gig." Oh God. Did I actually just say that out loud? I am hopeless.

Apparently Sari finds desperation to be attractive. Or, at least, she's not completely turned off. She spins, lays a hand on Yossi's forearm.

Sari Horowitz is voluntarily touching Yossi Gluck.

The Earth must be rotating backward on its axis. Even Yossi seems slightly bewildered by this fantastic turn of events. His cheeks flush pink, threatening the neck-splotch danger zone that I have come to know and fear.

"I had *no idea* you could play drums," she says, eyes wide with—can it really be?—admiration. "That's cool."

"Uhn. Mmh. Ahhg," Yossi grunts, and freezes. It's painful to watch. I know how he feels. Blink city.

Sari barely notices, though, flashing us one more smile. "See you in Elkin's class," she says to me, and then disappears in a thick cloud of flowery shampoo smell.

The bell rings sharply.

"Crap. We're late."

I glance at Yossi, but he hasn't heard a word I've said. Judging from the glazed look in his eyes, he's been hit with a wave of Sariliciousness. And he looks like he really, really liked it.

I nudge him forward, and he starts, stumbling more than walking, but at least we're moving forward. I'm hoping that Fogel will be so pleased by my new alliance with Yossi that she'll overlook the whole lateness thing, but I'm not really that worried. After that exchange with Sari,

Fogel could do just about anything but fail me and it'd probably bounce right off my back.

And I'm not the only one.

"I *am* sorry," I say, sneaking a glance at Yossi and noting with relief that the fever-haze has begun to subside. "For tricking you. Or pressuring you. Or both. *But,*" and here I actually stop for a moment and look him straight in the lust-struck eyeballs, "you have to admit that there are some *major* perks to being in a band."

He nods for a moment, mostly to himself. "Some," he admits at last. "Some."

And I know—for now, it doesn't matter that Yossi is feeling hurt and betrayed. It doesn't matter that for the most part, he's hardly the indie-rock type. Yossi is not impervious to that thing that we all want, that tiny grain of respect, that X factor that inspires shimmery, clean-smelling girls like Sari to reach out and tap you on the forearm. He's Yossi Gluck, yeah, but he's *human*, too. And I know I don't have to worry about keeping Yossi on board. Not for the immediate future, at least.

Which is something.

• • •

When my mother comes home from work, I'm sitting in our den, theoretically working on my math homework. In actuality I am alternately staring off into space and doodling in my Tribe notebook. I have written exactly one line of lyric since picking the notebook up (*Rainy day and*

I've / got nothing to say), but still feel like it was a good, solid purchase. The doodling is a nice distraction. Maybe too nice. I should be doing something to a parabola right now, if I have any hopes of sneaking in some guitar practice tonight.

"Oh, good, you're working," Mom says. She breezes in through the door that connects the garage to the den, moving across the room, hanging up her coat, laying her BlackBerry down on the kitchen counter, and resting her briefcase at the foot of the stairs, all in one smooth motion. Quite the multitasker, my mother.

"Yup." I slap my notebook shut and attempt to look very engrossed in focus derivations.

What the hell are focus derivations?

"I'm learning about *figurative language*," Ben pipes in from his corner of the room. "Like, if I were to tell you that I'm 'starving,' that would be figurative. Because I'm not *really* starving," he tells my mother.

"Thank God," I mutter. "I was worried for a minute there."

"But I am very hungry," he assures her quickly.

She smiles and crosses the room, ruffling his hair. "Dad's working late. Chinese is on the way."

"Yes!" Ben jumps out of his seat and does a little dance that involves gratuitous use of pointing. While he looks like a drug-addled freakshow, I can appreciate the sentiment. MSG may be technically kosher (I think), but in the Abramson household, it's as rare as a side of bacon.

The trilling of a cell phone shakes Ben out of his Dancing Without the Stars moment. You might not think that a socially-challenged eleven-year-old would have a need for a cell phone, but you'd be wrong. My parents gave it to him when he won the Gittleman Middle School BrainWars (don't ask), and he mainly uses it to call them while they're at work and give updates on his progress with homework.

Sad, isn't it?

I sit up in my seat. I've been so preoccupied with the walking disaster that shares my DNA, I didn't notice that he seems to have downloaded a new ringtone.

It's "Hava Nagilah."

As performed by the Tribe.

My eyes widen. "Ben!"

He shimmies toward me, catches my gaze, and raises his eyebrows in realization. He grabs the phone from the table, takes a quick glance at the display screen, and sends the call straight through to voicemail, do not pass go, do *not* let another note of that song ring within Shelly Abramson's earshot.

Once the phone is silenced, the room feels eerily still. A tiny charge runs up and down my spine. Did she hear? Did she notice? I mean, not that there's any way she'd know that the song was *my* band, *me* rocking out. But she might ask questions. And we can't have that.

"Ari," she says, taking advantage of the quiet.

Oh, man. This is it.

Goodbye, Tribe. Goodbye, gigs. Goodbye, rock-god dreams.

"I spoke to one of my partners today. His daughter is a Brandeis alum. Class of '99. She'd be happy to talk to you if you're interested in an informational interview."

An informational interview a year early, with an alumni who has no influence over the admissions board, for a school I don't want to go to. Awesome.

But at least my rock-god dreams remain, for the time being, intact.

"Mmm hmm," I mumble, hoping that I sound non-committal enough to appease her.

My non-response seems to do the trick. She heads out of the room and upstairs to change out of her work clothes, her second stop at the end of every day after making sure that Ben and I are academically on track.

Once she's gone, I allow myself to inhale deeply. I swallow air like it's water and I've been sunbathing on top of Mount Masadah.

Then I turn to Ben.

"*What*," I begin, my voice dangerously low, "was that?"

"What?" His eyes are almost as round as his cheeks.

"You know what."

"The ringtone?" He smiles hopefully, like maybe if he breaks out his cuteness big guns, I will be less likely to pummel him.

In this, he is incorrect.

I lean forward and grab at his sleeve. "Yes, the *ring-tone*," I hiss. "Where. Did. You. Get it?"

"Elana Mendel had it. She emailed it around to our class."

I do the mental mapping. Elana Mendel is Melissa Mendel's younger sister. Melissa Mendel is Sari Horowitz's best friend. Sari mentioned that Jonas was going to get her an MP3 of our show. Clearly he wasted no time in doing so. And it's already spread through Gittleman High, and is now making the rounds among our siblings.

That's really cool.

Except for the part where now Ben knows about the Tribe, and suddenly has the power to ruin my life.

Unless... unless he doesn't know that the Tribe is me. Or us. Or whatever.

"I didn't know you were in a *band*," he says breathlessly.

Right. Never mind, then.

"I'm not," I say. "I mean, well—just sometimes. It's a temporary thing." I'm stammering. The effect is not very suave. The good news, however, is that Ben seems majorly psyched about this new development. Which means that maybe—just maybe—his reverence for his punk-ass older brother will overshadow any life-ruining impulses that may crop up.

His eyes narrow. "Do Mom and Dad know?"

Or maybe not. "No." I glare at him. "And we're not going to tell them, are we?"

"What if I do?" he challenges. I have to give it to him—the kid's got some *cojones* on him tonight.

I think for a minute. Pizza's not going to do it this time. Ben's going to want something bigger in exchange for keeping my secret. And unfortunately, I have absolutely no leverage. I need him batting for team Tribe.

I've got it. "If you do, then they'll make me quit. And then you'll never be able to come to one of our gigs."

The corners of his mouth twitch into a slow smile. There's that look again—it is! It's reverence. I hit him squarely in the center of it. Never mind that as of right now, we don't actually have any other gigs.

As of right now, I'm safe. My secret is safe.

The Tribe is safe.

And that's what matters.

• • •

THE TRIBE HAS 54 FRIENDS

[SEE ALL FRIENDS]

COMMENTS [SHOWING 1 OF 12]

OMG! You guys are, like, sooo cool! When do we get to hear your next single? XOXO—*CampLara*

ADD COMMENT [see all comments]

THE STAR | ALL THE NEWS THAT'S FIT FOR FRAGILE YOUNG MINDS TO READ | NOV. 22, 2009

STUDENT FOCUS: "WE'RE WITH THE TRIBE"

STEVEN FOGEL
STAFF WRITER

THOSE OF US WHO WERE AT THE GITTLEMAN PEP RALLY LAST WEEK (AND THAT'S EVERYONE EXCEPT FOR MARK KAUFMAN AND JONATHAN JACOBS WHO WERE CAUGHT DRINKING WINE COOLERS IN THE BOY'S ROOM) KNOW THAT IN ADDITION TO A HEAVYWEIGHT LINEUP OF YESHIVA-DISTRICT BASKETBALL STARS, OUR STUDENT BODY NOW BOASTS A NEW ANTHEM TO RALLY BEHIND.

AND BELIEVE ME - THIS AIN'T YOUR RABBI'S MUSIC.

SURE, WE'VE ALL BEEN SINGING "HAVA NEGILA" SINCE OUR FIRST SIMCHAT TORAH SERVICE, BUT MOST OF US HAVE NEVER BEFORE HEARD IT PERFORMED WITH QUITE AS MUCH ENERGY.

ENTER THE TRIBE.

THE TRIBE CONSISTS OF THREE GITTLEMAN JUNIORS: FOUNDER AND SELF-PROFESSED JOE SCHMOE ARI ABRAMSON ON GUITAR, QUIET DARK HORSE YOSSI GLUCK ON DRUMS-(SERIOUSLY-DID ANY OF US SEE HIM COMING?), AND THE IRREPRESSIBLE JONAS FEIN ON BASS AND LEAD VOCALS. ROUNDING OUT THE QUARTET IS BACKUP SINGER REENA GLUCK WHOSE INIMITABLE VOCALS HAVE BEEN DESCRIBED AS A CROSS BETWEEN AMY WINEHOUSE AND A SANE PERSON.

THE TRIBE CAME TOGETHER BACK IN OCTOBER AND QUICKLY MADE A NAME FOR THEMSELVES PLAYING ROSS FEIN'S BAR MITZVAH - AND ROCKING THE JOINT. SINCE THEN, THEY'VE BEEN DILIGENTLY PRACTICING IN THE MUCH-DISCUSSED GLUCK RAQUETBALL COURT. "WE JOKE AROUND SOMETIMES AND CALL IT THE 'ROCKING-BALL COURT'," SAYS JONAS WITH A WINK. "I CAME UP WITH THAT. CAN YOU MAKE SURE THAT GOES IN THE ARTICLE? SERIOUSLY MAN, WHY AREN'T YOU WRITING THAT DOWN?"

CONSIDER IT ON THE RECORD, JONAS. *SF*

THE TRIBE (FROM LEFT): REENA GLUCK, JONAS FEIN, YOSSI GLUCK, ARI ABRAMSON

SEXY SHLOSS

BIRTHDAY: MAY 2ND, 1979
HOMETOWN: MILLBURN, NJ
PROFESSION: BIOLOGY TEACHER / VIXEN OF THE NIGHT

ABOVE: SCREENSHOT OF MS. SHLOSSBERG'S PROFILE

TEACHER FOUND, MOCKED ON FACEBOOK

(CONT. FROM PAGE 3)

GUESS I JUST FORGOT TO ADJUST MY PRIVACY SETTINGS."

SHLOSSBERG IS HUMBLED BY THE EXPERIENCE BUT TAKING IT IN STRIDE. "I'M THE TEACHER BUT I GUESS SOMETIMES IT'S THE TEACHER WHO LEARNS THE LESSON."

eight

Normally, I'd be completely freaked out to see the Tribe exposed in the *Gittleman Star*, our monthly school newspaper. But the good news is that the profile that appears in that particular issue is tucked well inside, back on page eight. As long as I don't go leaving my copy lying on the dining room table or anything like that, my parents won't see it. I can breathe easy.

Since our secret remains safe, I allow myself a nice, long bask as I skim through the article. Our progress may be... progressing in drips and drabs, but after two months we've had two gigs (that have passed without incident, for better or for worse), one wildly popular ringtone, and probably something like a billion practice sessions. I play as much as I can at home, which is more than you might think, since my parents are crazed workaholics and Ben is now on board with my secret. The fingers on my left hand are calloused and rough, which I love. It makes me feel hardcore.

We've got two new songs down now. "Lithium" (three chords, remember?), which sounds shivery and cool with a girl on backup vocals, and the Smith's "How Soon is Now?" It wouldn't be my choice for a Smiths cover, but Jonas insisted. He likes the t. A.T.u. version of it. Of course.

So yeah, we've almost got an entire set. A short set, but still a set. Which is a good thing, since we're coming up on our most important show ever.

Greg Schusterman's birthday.

As I may have mentioned, Greg Schusterman is kind of a big deal at Gittleman. He and Sari Horowitz used to go out, back in eighth grade, and they've stayed friends ever since they broke up (or so she says). Greg's birthday is in late November, so it almost always falls around Thanksgiving weekend. Which would normally be a bummer, but because Greg's parents are (a) rich and (b) sympathetic, they throw him a huge party every year before the break. It's in their rec room, which has shag carpeting, lava lights, and a pinball machine looming large in one corner.

Or so I hear. I've never actually been to a Greg Schusterman party. But that's about to change.

Remember how I had that idea about how being in a band would change my life? Well, it turns out I wasn't wrong. Because for the first time ever in my whole teenage life, I'm not only going to a Greg Schusterman party, but I'm going *as the main attraction.*

Well, the main attraction after Greg, that is.

"So, are we ready for Saturday night?" I ask, looking around the racquetball court.

Reena is lying on her stomach on the floor, resting her chin in her hands. She nods groggily. She thinks she's coming down with a cold. "Tea with honey," she says. "I'm all over it." I truly hope that she is. She sounds like she's speaking through wet cotton.

"I think gargling with saltwater is supposed to help, too," Yossi offers.

Gross.

"Yeah, but it's gross." She wrinkles her nose.

"We're on at ten," I say. "There isn't going to be a problem with the holy Sabbath, is there?"

Yossi shakes his head, even offers a small grin. "No. The sun'll be down by then. Shabbos is over."

I knew that. I must be more distracted by nerves than I realize.

"It's gonna be awesome," Jonas says. "Everybody loves us. But we have to be *cool.*"

Duh, I want to say. But then I look at Yossi, whose thick, curly hair is essentially fleeing his scalp in terror, and I realize that a little tutorial from Jonas Fein might actually be in order.

"Jeans," I say. I know for a fact Yossi has jeans. They're Dad-jeans-ish, but they're jeans. "And tee shirts." Yossi has been known to rock a mock turtleneck from time to time. Eeesh.

"Oh God"—Jonas cuts in, completely disregarding the fact that the phrase "oh God" makes Yossi wince—"and if you're going to wear a yarmulke, make it that rad one you got from Morocco. The tall one." He looks straight at Yossi, as though there could be any question as to who he's speaking to.

I've seen the yarmulke in question, by the way. It's seriously three inches high. It is pretty rad.

"And sneakers," Reena says, trying to keep her voice at a low whisper, all sexy musician–like. "Preferably of the non-athletic variety."

For a moment, a flicker of an expression makes its way across Yossi's face, and I wonder if he's pissed at being dressed, like he's a five-year-old. Then again, he owns a mirror. He must know what he looks like when he leaves the house in the morning.

Anyway, he needs to step it up. He's not just a foot soldier for the word of God these days. He's a rock star now. He has obligations, to us and to his fans. He needs to clean up. Which means guidance.

The moment passes and Yossi shrugs almost imperceptibly. He glances at his feet, which are loafer-shod. I kid you not. *Loafers.* Penny-free, thank God.

"I have sneakers," he says shortly, and turns back to his drum set.

This information does little to reassure me. I have to wonder—are we really ready? Greg Schusterman's birthday is, like, a whole other level for us.

It may take more than a pair of Vans and a few fake-vintage tees to rock that gig, kosher-style.

nine

Greg Schusterman's house is every bit the Eden of my dreams.

Mind you, I may be the eensiest bit biased, based on the fact that I've consumed approximately three seventeenths of a can of Michelob Extra Gold. So, technically, I'm under the influence. But still.

After three years of going to parties strictly as Jonas' sidekick (that is, when I go at all), I'm now here in official rock-god capacity. It's amazing, but also incredibly unreal (some of this could be the beer). I feel like an anthropologist on a jungle expedition, taking notes of my surroundings in vivid detail:

The shag carpet is a deep cerulean wool that scratches against the soles of my laceless Chuck Taylors. The lava lights in either corner of the wood-paneled rec room throw a pale purple pallor across the earnest, expectant faces of the party-goers. The room smells faintly of sour lite beer and nacho cheese powder.

Heaven. Right?

I feel a tap on my shoulder and turn to find Jonas. I hope for a moment that he hasn't seen me gawking like a kid at the zoo. Then I realize he's wearing sunglasses—inside, at ten-thirty on a Saturday night in November—and decide that I'm cool.

"We've gotta set up, man. We're on any f^&*ing minute."

Oh, yeah. The gig.

"Where are Yossi and Reena?" I ask. We'd separated upon arrival—Jonas was torn from us by a waiting female throng—and I haven't seen them since, mainly since I've been cowering behind the orange futon making like Margaret Mead.

Jonas points, first in one direction, then another. It's like Where's Waldo, except not hard. I spot our bandmates right away. They do both sort of stand out.

Yossi is off in another corner of the room, doing his best to become one with the blue corduroy beanbag chair that engulfs him. As advised, he wears the Moroccan yarmulke. It juts straight upward, providing a sharp contrast to the amorphous chair, and, well, to Yossi's body. He clutches a red plastic cup that probably contains water. I should go over to him, advise him in the ways of the three-seventeenths of a can. Help a brother out. But I have an idea that he wouldn't be easily persuaded.

For her part, Reena is sidled up to the long, paper-covered refreshment table, which she leans against with all of the grace of a salmon swimming upstream. A stray potato chip (ruffled, if you're curious) clings to the hem of her tiny tee shirt. I scan her face to see if I can read it—she's one part eager and excited, three parts nervous and worried. About what? That she's out of place?

I can relate.

I catch her eye and tilt my head in the general direction of our makeshift stage—a small circle of cleared space on the rug that has been spared the indignity of ground-up M&M's and puddles of overflowed Shasta Cola. She nods, stepping away from the food and brushing off the front of her shirt. It's a souvenir, I guess—her tee shirt. From a place called Wilbur's Chocolate. As unsexy as Wilbur's Chocolate sounds, she wears the shirt well. The girl looks good. Not unlike an indie chanteuse.

Jonas grabs Yossi and we wander somewhat hesitantly over to our instruments, taking our places for the performance. My throat feels hot and dry, and I wonder if anyone else is experiencing these symptoms. The Schustermans might want to look into investing in a humidifier down here.

For an acutely painful three minutes, we stand there,

looking and feeling awkward (or, at least, I feel awkward—I can't speak for anyone else). No one at the party seems to have noticed of us. They're all laughing and talking, waving all over the place while they tell each other wild stories and gesticulate like they're trying to land planes right here in Greg Schusterman's basement. None of us knows what to do.

Thankfully, we're rescued by Greg, who jumps in front of Jonas and grabs the mic from him. The room explodes in a shower of feedback that stops everyone in their tracks.

Now they're all looking at us.

I can't lie. I might have liked it better when they were making with the wild anecdotes and pretending that we didn't exist (if a band plays in the forest, but no one is around to hear it, is it possible for that band to suck?).

Relax, I tell myself. *You're not going to suck. These are your friends.*

Well, acquaintances.

Then the little voice in my mind speaks up. A lot of these people have had a lot more than I've had to drink—some have even finished whole entire cans of beer, all on their own! For some reason this calms me.

"Hey, guys," Greg says, grinning broadly at the room. "Thanks for, uh, coming out for my birthday."

Jeering, shrieks, and general mayhem ensue.

"So . . . we've, uh, got a band tonight."

Milder mayhem.

"This is . . . " He pauses dramatically. "TRIBUTE!"

The mayhem sputters a last death rattle.

Satisfied with his less-than-impressive lead-in, Greg passes the mic to me, staggering forward and away from us, still beaming madly at the crowd.

And it is a crowd. I mean, it's maybe thirty kids, which is fewer people than we played for at the bar mitzvah, but in this case, the stakes feel higher. Maybe 'cause we're in a room full of our peers, not just playing for rabbinical school dropouts, thirteen-year-olds, and other miscellaneous types. And this ain't no Gittleman pep rally—this is *Greg Schusterman's* house. This is big-time. These people's approval actually means something.

Or it will, if we earn it.

I take a breath and try to loosen my shoulders, grasping at the microphone. My hands feel dangerously slippery. Why can't Right Guard do something for that?

"Yeah," I say, leaning into the mic. "We're actually—"

The microphone is yanked out of my hands by a zealous Jonas, who brings it up to his mouth and practically devours it. "We're the *f^&*ing* TRIBE!"

He has managed to work up another frenzy, this one almost matching Greg's. I'm impressed. And also, relieved.

Jonas nods at Yossi. Yossi nods to himself. He mouths a countdown so only we can see.

Then he just loses his whole damn mind. And he takes us with him.

• • •

We play our whole set list, of course. I mean, it's a short list: "Lithium" (our tightest, by far; much love and respect to KC); "How Soon Is Now?"; and "Hava Nagilah." Strangely, that's the one that people really get into. I don't know, maybe it's in their roots or something. Then we launch into a bare-bones "Happy Birthday" for Greg, which ends with Jonas doing his best Bret Michaels and cursing a lot. Shocking, I know.

By the time we finish, I feel like a towel that someone has wrung out and left on the clothesline. Limp and empty. Reena finds me sunk deep into a bean bag chair, sweating profusely (always a good look).

"Here." She presses a blessedly cool can of—regular—Coke into my hand.

"Thank you," I say, running the can over my forehead. "Seriously."

She collapses onto the floor next to me and settles herself into a cross-legged position. "We were good," she says. It's not a question.

She pulls her hair into a thick, messy bun at the base of her neck. I think she feels as droopy as I do, she just droops a whole lot better. Her cheeks are tinged pink. Her eyes sparkle. She's glowing. I'm reminded of those Renaissance paintings where the saints are all alight with receiving the word of God and all.

"We were tight," I agree. "I was a half a beat behind during the second chorus of 'How Soon is Now,' though."

"I don't think anyone noticed," she assures me.

I didn't think so either, but positive reinforcement is always welcome.

"They were totally focused on Jonas," she goes on.

I frown.

Is this it, then? My so-called grab for top billing? Like, is Jonas always going to overshadow me?

On the one hand, when he's around, I'm about fifty percent less spazzy. But on the other hand, that's probably due in large part to the fact that, when he's around, I'm about fifty percent more unnoticed.

It's tricky.

"Dude, we f^&*ing *rocked.*" Jonas saunters over, gives me an overly enthusiastic five.

Ow.

"That is a true fact," Reena states primly. But she's still smiling and shiny in that good way. It idly occurs to me that in her post-set afterglow, Reena could even give Sari Horowitz a run for her money.

"That. Was. *Awesome.*"

Speaking of Sari.

"It" was. And "it" is. Awesome. Both our set, which is what Sari's referring to, and also my ability to conjure her presence using only the powers of my mind. Awesome. In the literal, Biblical sense of the word.

Sari flings one arm around Jonas' neck, clinking her beer against the back of his long-sleeved tee shirt. "Ohmigod."

"Shh," he whispers, teasing. He holds his index finger

to his lips. "Yossi'll f^&*ing *freak* if you take the lord's name in vain."

Sari collapses into giggles. I kind of want to stab myself in the eye. Myself, or Jonas.

Mostly Jonas.

"Yossi has been pantomime-drumming to himself for the last twenty-seven minutes," Reena clarifies. "Ever since we finished our set." She pushes herself to her feet languidly, shakes out her arms. "This is not quite his element. I think I'm going to go put him out of his misery." She turns to me. "Do you need a ride home?"

Do I? I glance at Jonas, who is not even remotely glancing at me. In fact, Jonas is holding Sari Horowitz's left hand, manipulating her delicate, French-tipped fingers into the position for A minor.

Sari pauses momentarily. "Melissa has her car, if you want a ride," she says. "Later."

She's talking to Jonas, not me.

I nod to myself, taking the scene in. I'm frustrated. I want to say that now that Jonas is Gittleman High's answer to Joel Madden, the student has surpassed the master, and yeah, it's driving me out of my head.

But I know better. The truth is, Jonas was never the student. *I* was the student. Jonas was the master. And for now, the status quo remains firmly in place.

"Yeah," I say to Reena. "I need a ride."

• • •

THE TRIBE HAS 68 FRIENDS
[SEE ALL FRIENDS]

COMMENTS [SHOWING 2 OF 37]

Saw your gig this weekend and you rocked! I'm with the Tribe.—*Gittleguy*

You. Were. Awesome. Ohmigod.—*Sari-licious42*

ADD COMMENT [see all comments]

• • •

A weird thing happens on Tuesday night. I'm in my room, theoretically looking over sample essays from past SATS, but really cruising the Tribe's MySpace profile and obsessing over how many friends we have (kind of a lot, considering), when there's a knock on the door.

This is unusual for two, not unrelated, reasons: firstly, that my parents, who are assiduous knockers (they're sticklers for privacy), are out at a dinner with some friends (this happens rarely, and is an occasion which I, as an independence-minded teenage guy, must savor); and also that Ben, who is in fact home, could give a rat's ass about my so-called privacy. Ben has some serious entitlement issues.

"Come in," I say, incredibly curious about the turn of events. Of course, it wouldn't take a whole lot to distract me from fake SAT studying. I collapse the telltale MySpace window on my computer screen.

It's Ben. Which makes sense, since, as I mentioned, he's the only person here right now. But his entire demeanor is off. It's like he's been replaced by a pod-person, or a brother-bot. Some sort of Ben 2.0 cyborg.

"Hey," he says, swaying slightly back and forth in the door frame. From my perch at my desk, he looks small and slightly vulnerable.

"Hey?" I'm slightly impatient. I've got test-prep work to not do, after all. And Greg Schusterman's party to relive in my mind. Over and over again. Unless his swaying is a sign of low blood sugar or something, I'm not interested.

"I, um, wanted to ask you something." He looks mortified, and I feel a flash of panic at wondering what sort of thing he may want to ask me that would cause him this much shame. I am, after all, a big brother, however nominally.

I am *really* not prepared to do "The Talk" with Ben. Birds, bees, and other incredibly intimate things of which I have no real knowledge. Gah. I mean, I think a person needs a little firsthand experience before he is qualified to speak as an expert, you know? Not that I'm totally unfamiliar with the female anatomy, but let's just say…

You know what? Let's just not say. Not right now, anyway. I mean, my private life is no one's business but my own.

Then again, those who can't do, teach, right? At least

I'm finally master, rather than student, even if fraudulently so. It had to happen sometime.

I channel my inner role model. It requires digging deep. My inner role model has been latent, if not completely non-existent, up until now.

"Shoot," I say, smiling in what I hope is an open and inviting manner.

It feels like my lips are curling back from my teeth sort of feral-like, but whatever I'm doing, it seems to work. Ben stops mid-sway and grabs onto the doorway on either side of himself, pitching forward slightly. His shirt rides up over his stomach. I want to rush forward and give him a frontal wedgie, but as this would not be role model behavior, I exert a little bit of self control.

"CnIavyrautogrph?" he mumbles.

At first I'm not sure that I've heard him, or that he's even really said anything. Like, maybe he just burped up something particularly rancid or something. "Huh?" I cock my hand over my ear in the universal "speak up" gesture.

"Can I"—he kicks his right foot out and then brings it back to his body—"have your autograph?"

My eyes threaten to bug out of my head. "My *autograph*?" The kid inherited my entire middle school library. He could fill an entire bookshelf with books emblazoned with my preteen John Hancock. Though I seriously can't imagine why he would. "What for?"

"Ben Birnbaum offered me a slice of his pizza lunch tomorrow if I get it for him."

Ah, pizza. Like cigarettes in prison. The currency of the sixth grade. Well, at least I can respect that. "Uh..." I rummage around in the top drawer of my desk for a piece of scrap paper. "Sure..." I pause, glance at Ben. "Wait a second."

He looks nervous. Busted.

"I thought Ben Birnbaum moved to Cherry Hill last August?"

Ben looks like he wants to barf. He squeezes his shoulders together tightly, shuts his eyes, and then opens them. "Okay," he confesses, exhaling in a big *whoosh.* "It's for me."

"I'm going to have to go with, *huh?*"

Ben flushes, and finally stumbles forward out of the doorway and into my room. He perches on my bed, legs swinging an inch above the floor. "Everyone knows about your gig on Saturday."

I have to admit, it's a little bit cute to hear him use the word *gig.*

"I heard you guys rocked." His eyes are wide and wet.

"We did," I agree. False modesty never did anyone any good.

"Do you think..." he starts shyly, sitting on his hands and swinging his feet vigorously, "that maybe I could come to one of your shows sometime?"

Is this what it feels like to be a role model? Like an actual, outer role model? Because I have to admit, it feels kind of... nice. Like there's a ball of something other than dread and anxiety gummed up inside of my chest.

I wonder if real rock stars feel this way *all of the time.* Because I could really get used to it.

• • •

I'm on fire tonight. It's like the elements have convened in such a way that everything is coming together for me. To wit, just moments after Ben leaves my room, waving a freshly-signed Post-it note in the air triumphantly (he's very concerned about the ink smearing—apparently it affects the potential resale value of the autograph or something), the following exchange goes down:

SARILICIOUS42: U AROUND?

ILIKELOUREED: SUPPOSED TO BE STUDYING.

SARILICIOUS42: I JUST ASSUMED U'D BE WORKING ON NEW SONGS & STUFF. ;)

ILIKELOUREED: I SAID "SUPPOSED" TO BE STUDYING, RIGHT?

SARILICIOUS42: GOTCHA. WELL, IF U FEEL LIKE DOING REAL WORK SOMETIME, I'VE GOT A PROPOSITION FOR U.

ILIKELOUREED: ?

SARILICIOUS42: I NEED HELP IF I'M GOING TO PASS CALC. ANY CHANCE I COULD GET U TO TUTOR ME?

Um, survey says: hell, yeah. I knew the parents' MATH! craze would someday prove useful to me.

Must. Be. Cool.

ILIKELOUREED: I'D SAY THERE'S A PRETTY GOOD CHANCE. BUT I DON'T COME CHEAP.

SARILICIOUS42: OF COURSE NOT. WHAT IF I PROMISED TO BE UR #1 FAN? WOULD THAT BE PAYMENT ENOUGH?

ILIKELOUREED: HMM ... #1 FAN. SOUNDS KIND OF STALKERISH.

SARILICIOUS42: IN A GOOD WAY?

Like Sari stalking me could *ever* be taken in anything but a good way.

I mean, really.

We make a deal. We're going to meet once a week after school until finals. Our arrangement works for me.

Hell, yeah.

MARKOWITZ DARED ME TO DO THE STUPIDEST THING I COULD THINK OF. JONAS FEIN NEVER TURNS DOWN A DARE. HE SHOULD BE HERE WITH MY $5 ANY MINUTE.
CRAZY GLUE YOUR HAND TO YOUR LOCKER?
ACTUALLY, HE SHOULD'VE BEEN HERE THREE HOURS AGO. DAMMIT MARK-OWITZ, YOU'VE FOOLED ME AGAIN!
RIGHT, UM... I'LL GET THE NURSE.
SNAP!!
WHAT THE HELL...
...WAS THAT??

THAT KID WAS LIKE TWELVE.
PAPARAZZI
YEAH, I KNOW, BLAME THE INTERNET
LUNCH
MAD
MAXIM
XXOO LARA M CAMP
A TALE OF TWO ITIES

OH, SPEAKING OF PUBLICITY, CHECK OUT THESE GLAM SHOTS I PUT TOGETHER OF THE BAND.
WE WEREN'T SPEAKING OF PUBLICITY BUT WHATEVER
HOMEWORK BAND SHIT
THIS IS NOT A GLAM SHOT. THIS IS MY 7TH GRADE CLASS PHOTO SCOTCH-TAPED TO A J CREW AD.
THE PEOPLE AT THE METRO-WEST JEWISH WEEKLY COULDN'T TELL THE DIFFERENCE.
MY MOM READS THAT PAPER.

OH DEAR LORD!
HEY, ARE YOU STILL GONNA GET THE NURSE?!

ten

So.

It was bound to happen sooner or later. And yet, when it does, I still react—still feel, oddly, distant and wounded at the same time. Like on the one hand, whatever's happening is not quite happening to *me,* and on the other hand, it definitely frickin' smarts.

Jonas is becoming an asshole.

Again, this is not hugely shocking; he was always sort of an ass. So the extra leap to "ass*hole*" was an imminent threat. But there somehow has always been a fine line between the jackass who schools me in PS4 most afternoons and the total freak of nature who has taken to wearing sunglasses *all* *the time.* Like he's just had surgery on his eyes, or he's got a perpetual hangover. Or like he's just too goddamn rock 'n' roll to deal.

He's the pop-punk version of Medusa. He wears those lame glasses for our protection; without them, he'd turn us to stone with his disaffected faux-emo glare. Medusa, or the ghost of a blonde pop princess. And he doesn't know from faux; he thinks of himself as a genuine musician, if not an actual *artiste.* Gah.

He's been writing songs, too. Okay, I know I've spent more time drawing imaginary scenarios of rock superstardom in my notebook than actual lyrics, but still—the way I see it, that's *my* role. Any day now, inspiration could hit.

For me, I mean. Inspiration could hit for *me.* Jonas is plenty "inspired" as it is. He has been known to concoct entire stanzas out of that dusty old classic rhyme combo: *bright/light.* Remember what I was saying about pop music? Jeez. It would be sad, if he weren't buying into his own hype these days.

It's entirely possible that he's sold his soul for those stupid sunglasses. Which may or may not have been a fair trade.

You might have noticed that my annoyance levels are high. I mean, I'd be worried if you hadn't. Noticed, that is. I think it was Greg Schusterman's party that sent me spiraling into this state of semi-acute existential crisis. Like I say, there was this rush that came with rocking out in front of a room full of kids whose opinions, you know, *matter* somehow (even if I deeply, constantly, wish that they don't). But there was also a corresponding rush of energy, anti-matter or something, that came from feeling like we're all just bit players in the movie of Jonas' life. A Greek chorus that will never be as memorable, as indelible, as the mainstage thespian of the production.

You get where I'm going with this, right?

The bitchier Jonas behaves at practices ("I think we need to write more original songs, man … I mean, your songs are, like, your *children* … they need to be nurtured, and … written"), the quieter Yossi grows. I expect him to melt away completely sometime between now and Israeli Independence Day. But at least he's not doing anything negative per se. Anything to upend the status quo. Such behavior wouldn't be in the spirit of the Holy One (blessed be he), I presume.

The same cannot, sadly, be said for Reena, who becomes edgier and more prickly by the nanosecond. The tips of her braids seem jagged and pointy, dangerous somehow, and her eye makeup is increasingly smudgy and dark. It's all very early-grunge Courtney Love, but without the heroin addiction (I mean, I think). She doesn't even bother anymore with her short, clipped standard—"*wo*man"—when Jonas launches into his impassioned creative genius, *"man"* tirades. I wonder what Haruki Murakami would have to say about that.

(Yes, I've been reading Murakami. No, I'm not sure I'm understanding it. There are a lot of people trapped at the bottom of wells, and communicating from telephones in a different time-space continuum and stuff. Weird.)

One thing I can say for sure about Murakami, he's definitely a writer who doesn't believe in limits. His story flips back and forth between cultures, perspectives, timeframes. None of it is very linear.

It's kind of the opposite of calculus.

Calculus, paradoxically, is mostly about limits. And integers, and derivatives, and infinite series. And I'm not any kind of savant when it comes to this sort of stuff, but it sure makes a lot more sense to me than wacky new-age fiction does. Yeah, I know people are always wondering when they're going to use this high school stuff in real life, and I'm totally one of those people, but for today, I kind of don't care. I could give a crap if the sum of two integers is something that never, ever, comes up in my life again. Because I'm using it *now*. Today. To tutor Sari.

If only our session were an infinite series. For that, I'd take AP math *ad infinitum.* The trick would be talking Sari into going along with the plan with me. Or, let's be honest, *for* me.

"I don't get it," she says. She wrinkles her nose. I'm pretty sure she doesn't want to get it, really, but I guess that as long as she keeps wrinkling her nose intermittently, we'll be okay. It's a good nose, even all scrunched up. *Especially* all scrunched up.

I pause, tap my pen against our dining room table. (Sari Horowitz is sitting at the Abramson dining room table! If I could only somehow talk her into eating or drinking something other than bottled water and Extra sugar-free gum, it would almost be like we'd shared a meal. In a datey way, I mean.)

"Let's talk about functions," I say, and then instantly want to stab myself in the temple with my Bic erasable pen for sounding inexcusably excited at the prospect of just that.

What is the opposite of hard-to-get? Like, maybe, won't-go-away? Yeah, that's me.

She snaps away at her gum, louder than Rice Krispies in milk. The scent of slightly dulled Wintermint wafts toward me. It's intoxicating. "When's your next gig?"

Good question. "Not sure," I say, trying to sound cool and noncommittal as opposed to has-been-y. "We're working on some stuff."

"Yeah." Her eyes are wide and sparkly, like I imagine Wintermints would be if they were a real thing that existed in nature. "Jonas told me you guys are, like, *exploding*. Onto the scene. It's so cool." She actually bats her eyelashes at me, like it's the forties and we're starring in some sexy, dimly lit film noir. "Will you promise to remember me when you're all famous?"

Um, yeah.

"Done," I say. I consider winking, then toss that plan on the grounds that by the time I'm done considering it, I've definitely missed my moment. If I ever even had a moment to begin with.

"I could be a groupie." She giggles.

Um, yeah.

"I could carry stuff."

I grin. "You know, Sari," I say, sounding a little cheesy and full of crap even to my own ears, "some of that equipment is really heavy."

"I'm strong!" She flexes, makes a muscle that's almost as adorable as her nose, mid-wrinkle. She's wearing a dark pink tee shirt over a longer-sleeved, lighter shirt, and the fabric stretches daintily over her limb as she tenses mid-pose.

Pink is definitely my new favorite color.

"Anyway," she continues, uncurling her forearm and casually rearranging the folds of her clothing now that our bodybuilding session is apparently over, "I already told Jonas. I promised I'd help him *schlep* his stuff. You know, his bass."

Schlep is Yiddish (old-school Jewish-speak) for "drag around." But we can't focus on that now.

What we need to focus on right now is the fact that Sari has evidently attached herself to our as-yet-unscheduled world tour. I mean, that's awesome news, right? That's so punk rock.

Almost as punk rock as pining over the girl who's pining over your best friend.

Right. So, yeah. What I need to get back to is the good news buried in all of that quasi mind-blowing, sensory-overloading information. Before stabbing myself in the temple with an erasable pen begins to look like a reasonable option again.

It's all about limits. In Calculus, in indie bands, in

high school … in life. In just about everything—except for a particular oeuvre of Japanese literature, really—limits are key. And I might be creeping, tentative but righteously, toward the edge of mine.

• • •

Okay, so: you know what's lamer than lusting after some extremely generic (if inexplicably hot) girl who is so into your friend that she's actually resorted to reviving a semi-dead language?

Hanging out with your eleven-year-old kid brother. *Voluntarily.*

Teaching him guitar, specifically.

Apparently I really *don't* have any limits. Who knew?

Thanksgiving weekend descends on me with the subtlety of an avalanche, and just as cold and dark. Jonas and his family are skiing in Aspen, and I have no idea what the Glucks are up to (though if I had to bet on Yossi, I'd give even-odds that he's running a Torah discussion group somewhere). Mom and Dad, of course, don't believe in breaks, so after some perfunctory turkey with Aunt Minna and Uncle Sol, they're off to the office again, working. Leaving Ben and me alone in the house, all day every day.

They don't call it "Black Friday" for nothing. It's a lot of quality time.

I'm flash-carded out, and now Mom wants me to focus on some practice essays for the creative portion of the SATs but that's ... not gonna happen. At least, not if she's spending ten-ish hours a day at the office. That's ten-ish hours that are completely my own. *Ten hours.*

It's no surprise that I'm so bored I want to rip out all of the pages in my ever-expanding notebook, toss them up into the air, and see about re-arranging all of my dumb little doodles into an entirely new story line. Like a flip book. Or a Mad Libs. Of my non-life.

I finish *The Wind-Up Bird Chronicle* and move on to *Kafka on the Shore.* I thought it was one I'd heard of before, something about killing some guy, a total stranger on the beach, and then I start it and realize the two are completely separate stories. I was thinking of Camus, *The Stranger.* Totally different esoteric reflection on the absurdity of the human condition. But anyway, I tell Mom it's for AP English, extra credit reading, and buy myself a brief stay of execution re: SAT essaying. To do ... nothing, I guess, except scan idly through a novel I'm 86 percent sure I don't get. And teach Ben guitar.

"*That* is not A minor!" he shrieks, batting my fingers away from his own. He clutches the guitar—*my* guitar—to his chest possessively and gives the strings a good, enthusiastic strum. The amp squeals and the edges of my teeth vibrate. "A minor is more like a bear claw." He poses his hand tensely outward, letting it float at eye level with me.

"I didn't realize you were going for a modernist interpretation of the hand placement," I say. He's like Van Gogh. Or someone *really* off his head.

"It's from *Guitar for Dummies,*" he sniffs. I'd be embarrassed for him, except that I've got *The Everything Guitar Book* stashed in an abandoned corner of my closet. Sad.

The house phone rings, shocking both of us. Ben promptly places his index finger on the tip of his nose, a "not-it" gesture from back before I honed my big brother strong arm tactics.

"Go." I shove him. "It could be Mom."

He races off to the nearest extension, which happens to be in our parents' bedroom. I hear my guitar banging against his thighs as he runs. If he so much as scratches the face of that thing, I might have to shave his head in his sleep. Or something better. Less traceable.

"ARI!" He is clearly not afraid to project from the diaphragm. You'd think there was a nuclear meltdown going on in the bedroom, that's how urgent and panicky he sounds.

"God, *what*?" I ask, gasping a little bit as I slow to a halt in the doorway. "*Jeez.*"

He holds the phone out. "It's for you." He covers the mouthpiece, thirty-four kinds of discretion. "A *girl.*"

Sari doesn't strike me as the type who'd want to cram some extra calc-time in over a holiday, but I give my brain a beat or two to go wild with that scenario before wrenching the receiver out Ben's hand. He stomps off, staring, fixated, at a hand configuration that, to be fair, can really only be described as a bear claw. Those *Dummies* could be on to something.

"Hello?"

"Ari?"

It *is* a girl! And she sounds kind of familiar. Since there are exactly two people of the feminine persuasion who have ever called me at home, one of whom gave birth to me sixteen years ago, I'm still thinking this could be Sari with some kind of cold, or hideous affliction of the vocal chords.

"Yeah, what's up?" I'm suave, like a person who fields all sorts of calls from many, many woman—most of whom are not related to him—every day.

"It's Reena."

Oh. *Oh.*

I forgot I do know another girl. But I'm excused from that momentary blip because it's not like we run around being all friendly all the time or anything, outside of Tribe stuff.

"Hey. What's up?"

"You said that already."

Of course I did. Someone who spends more time on the phone with girls wouldn't have made that error. Rookie mistake.

"Yeah, well... you never answered." *Touché.*

"Touché," she says. "Not much. What have you been doing?"

"Practicing, you know," I say, shrugging my shoulders and then realizing that she can't see me over the phone. "Reading."

"Yeah?" Is it my imagination, or has that got her interest? "What are you reading?"

"*Kafka—*" I pause, realizing that for some weird reason that's not apparent even to me, I don't want her to know about my newest little flirtation with Murakami. "Kafka. Uh, *The Metamorphosis.*" Great. So she doesn't know I've been stalking her book club of one, but she does think I'm a pretentious freak.

All of which begs the question: why do I care?

"I don't care," I say, then realize I'm still on the phone.

"About Kafka?" She's confused—understandably, seeing as how she still inhabits the world of rational people who have grasped basic social skills. She laughs. "Yeah, screw Kafka!"

I can't help it. I laugh too.

"So, it was Yossi's birthday," she goes on, making me feel a complicated mixture of guilt, ambivalence, and anxiety for not having known.

"Oh," I say. "I thought you guys were ... " I have no idea. I sink down onto the armchair adjacent to my parents' bed. Talking to Reena is exhausting, though I don't know why. I change tracks. "What'd you do?"

"Well, get this," she says eagerly. "My parents got him a Jeep!"

I am now, officially, the only member of the Tribe who doesn't have a car (not to mention a license). Why does God hate me? Is it because of that time Brian Farber dared me to eat a ham and cheese sandwich after soccer practice in third grade? Because, I mean, I got food poisoning from that sandwich, and wound up puking all over a pop vocab test. So, you know, I think it's safe to say I've atoned and it's all ancient history. I, for one, am totally over it, *God.*

"That's cool," I say, wondering if she can hear how tightly my jaws are clenched. Is jealousy punk rock or not? I'm really not sure.

"It's gonna be great, you know, for hauling equipment and stuff. Like to gigs," she gushes, delicately avoiding the fact that we have exactly 0.0 gigs booked on the horizon. I've been thinking of putting in a bid for the Tribe to play at the Purim Prom, that's how desperate I am.

"But anyway, that's not really why I called," she says, exhaling her words all in a big rush, like she's in a hurry to get to her own point. "See, there's . . . this show."

A *show* is a concert, remember?

"Who's playing?" I ask, before it occurs to me that I might think about being at least *sort of* cool about the whole thing. I'm really not sure where she's going with this.

"Love and Sprockets," she says.

I wonder if she knows that I just downloaded their new single. She must know. We're in a band together. She knows my taste. That's why she's even telling me about this, to begin with.

Wait—*why* is she even telling me about this, to begin with? The show is definitely not in Essex county, NJ. I mean, it's in the city (Manhattan, to you). It's got to be. And the trains are not exactly walking distance.

Still: Love and Sprockets.

"Where's the show?" I ask.

She names a grungy closet on the outermost border of the lower east side. Right. The city.

"I was thinking we could go."

Hey. Okay. Is she, uh, asking me out? Like, if we were going to a show together, would that be a date? I think for a minute—I've never actually been on a proper, one-girl-one-guy, no best friends, pizza, board games, or crappy-blockbuster-group-movie outings involved. My one-to-one ratio action has been strictly limited to tutoring Sari Horowitz, and as much I'd love for those to be considered real dates, I know that they aren't. Just … no.

Not to Sari, anyway.

Do I *want* to go on a date with Reena? I'm not sure. The one solid fact that I have at my fingertips is that, apparently, I don't even want to tell Reena that I'm reading her favorite author. Which in this context makes the whole date thing seem … not so smart. At best.

I grab a pencil off the writing table beside me and sketch a bare-bones version of my Fender on the notepad Mom keeps out for phone messages and stuff. It's soothing.

I almost forget that I'm even on the phone, contemplating the possibility of dateyness with Reena, when she breaks into my thoughts.

" … so Yossi says he'll drive."

Yossi? Yossi's driving? Yossi's *coming?*

Not a date, then.

"Oh," I say weakly. "Cool."

Which it is, actually. If I hadn't just experienced every possible nuance of human emotion in the course of seventeen seconds, I might be more upbeat about it all.

Ben. What about Ben? It won't be looked kindly on if I leave him at home to fend for himself. And I don't trust him alone with my guitar, either.

I formulate a plan. I can ship him off on a sleepover at Matt Sherman's house. Good old Matt Sherman and his incredibly accommodating mother.

"Jonas is in, too," Reena adds.

With every word out of her mouth, the entire expedition's date-like qualities decrease exponentially. I have to wonder why I'm suddenly sort of bummed about that.

"Wait a minute," I say, remembering. "Jonas was supposed to be visiting Larafr—*Lara* when he got back from Aspen. Isn't he with her now?"

"Yeah, no, he's home," Reena chirps. There's a crunching sound, like she's scarfing down some chips or something while we talk. Which makes the last vestige of romantic mystique just dry right up and out of this phone call. "I don't know. Whatever. We'll pick you up at eight!" She hangs up.

I meditate for a moment on the dial tone, then hang up, too. She'll pick me up at eight. With Yossi and Jonas. For our plans which are not a date. With the girl who is not my crush. And two guys who are seriously getting on my nerves lately, each for entirely different reasons.

The whole thing reeks of bad-idea-itis. But, as Jonas would say, what the f^&*? Yeah, I'm in.

It's too late not to be in, and besides, wasn't I just going on about the end-stage vacation cabin fever and stuff? Boredom can be a powerful motivator, obviously.

So I'm in, then. I mean, it beats SAT studying. I guess.

eleven

"Dude, man, f^&*ing crank up the *tunes*!"

Jonas' voice from the back seat of Yossi's car is exactly as irritating as Ben's attempts to master an A minor chord. Where before my teeth were on edge, now I think my eyeballs are. They roll in my head like they're super-charged with electrical power.

A wiry hand reaches over the arm rest and I slap it away. "We are listening. To. The Black Angels."

I hate the Black Angels. But so does Jonas. Shotgun has its perks.

"I hate the Black Angels." From bitch position, Reena

thrusts a CD into my hands. She graciously offered to take that spot after Ben pitched a fit en route to Matt Sherman's, but hasn't moved over since we dropped him off. Now there's a big, empty, Ben-shaped space directly to her left, while she's practically sitting on Jonas' lap. I know she's not into him, though. She's like the only one who isn't—too smart. What can I say? She's a strange one. I glare at her, then eject the Black Angels and shove her disc in.

It's Neko Case. The wrong Nico, but still.

She nods her head. "It's the wrong Nico, but still." She hums a little bit, getting into the music.

Unimpressed by the shoegazey soundtrack, Jonas inhales like a coke fiend on Ritalin. "New car smell."

I doubt he's fawning over Yossi's birthday gift just to piss me off, or make me jealous, but I kind of want to punch him in the face anyway. I'm grouchy tonight.

"It's new," Yossi duhs. Except he doesn't mean it as a duh. He means it sincerely. Yossi means everything sincerely. It's a problem.

"Why didn't you tell us it was your birthday, man?" Jonas asks. "We could have partied. Larafromcamp's got friends. I bet some of them even go for that *frum*-y, ortho thing." Meaning how Yossi's all religious and stuff.

"Hnnuh." Even Yossi's stammering is sincere. That takes heart.

"Whatever. This *rocks.* I can't wait to get to the Alley Cat."

He's talking about the club. "It's the Back Alley,"

THE BACK ALLEY, LOWER EAST SIDE, NEW YORK CITY
S**T MAN, THIS PLACE IS F^&*ING AWESOME! CHECK OUT ALL THESE ROCKER CHICKS ARI MAN! OH MAN, THAT CHICK WITH THE DRAGON TATTOO IS TOTALLY CHECKING ME OUT.

FOR F^&*'S SAKE, DON'T YOU HAVE A F^&*ING GIRLFRIEND?! CAN'T WE JUST WATCH THE F^&*ING SHOW?!
HEATMISER

UM, WE INTERRUPT THIS EPISODE OF CHILDISH BEHAVIOR TO BRING YOU THIS: YOSSI IS MISSING.

NO, DON'T WORRY, I SAW HIM OUTSIDE TALKING TO THE BOUNCER ABOUT SOME LAME S**T.
HEATMISER

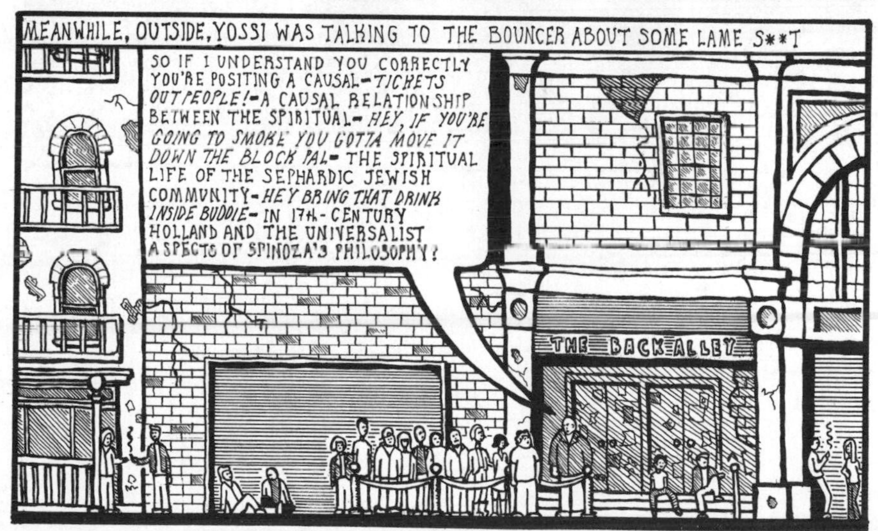
MEANWHILE, OUTSIDE, YOSSI WAS TALKING TO THE BOUNCER ABOUT SOME LAME S**T
SO IF I UNDERSTAND YOU CORRECTLY YOU'RE POSITING A CAUSAL—*TICKETS OUT PEOPLE!*—A CAUSAL RELATIONSHIP BETWEEN THE SPIRITUAL—*HEY, IF YOU'RE GOING TO SMOKE YOU GOTTA MOVE IT DOWN THE BLOCK PAL*—THE SPIRITUAL LIFE OF THE SEPHARDIC JEWISH COMMUNITY—*HEY BRING THAT DRINK INSIDE BUDDIE*—IN 17th-CENTURY HOLLAND AND THE UNIVERSALIST ASPECTS OF SPINOZA'S PHILOSOPHY?
THE BACK ALLEY

WELL, MORE OR LESS. IT'S JUST ONE WAY OF SAYING THAT THE PATHS OF SPIRITUALITY AND OF PURE REASON ULTIMATELY LEAD TO THE SAME PLACE.

HEH. WELL, I KNOW A FEW ANCIENT GREEKS WHO MIGHT BEG TO DIFFER BUT YOU HAVE SOME INTERESTING IDEAS. IF YOU GIVE ME YOUR EMAIL ADDRESS I'LL SEND YOU THE NAMES OF SOME BOOK'S YOU'LL ENJOY.

WHAT THE?!... YOSSI?!
IMPROV NIGHT
THE POSSESSIONS
SOLD OUT!

OH, HEY REENA. I WAS JUST MAKING SMALL TALK WITH LEONARD HERE.
UGH, NOT SPINOZA AGAIN...
ANTS

LEONARD, THIS IS MY SISTER, REENA. WE CAME HERE WITH OUR BAND TO SEE LOVE AND SPROCKETS.

HEH, WHEN I WAS YOUR AGE I WAS IN A BAND WITH MY SISTER TOO!

WE LIVED IN A TWO-ROOM APARTMENT ON AVENUE D WITH THREE OTHER CATS.
THE WHO

I BET YOU KIDS GET INTO ALL SORTS OF TROUBLE WITH THE NEIGHBORS.

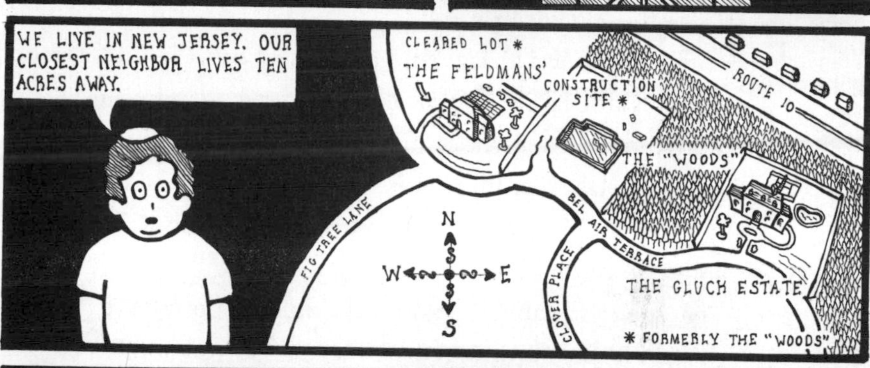

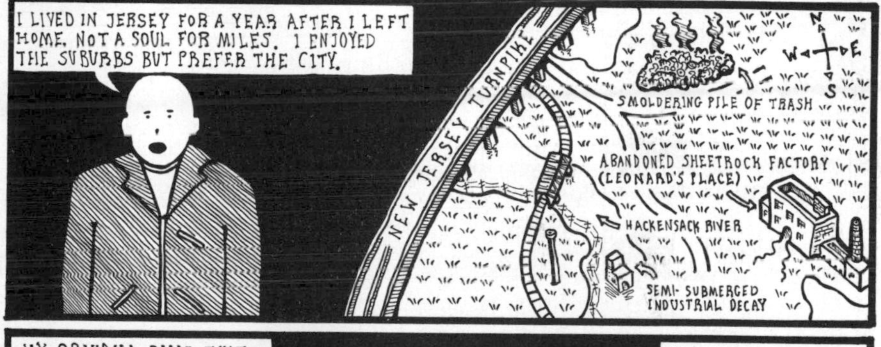

Reena and I say simultaneously. I catch her eye in the rear-view mirror; she sneers at me, then winks.

"I heard that actor, you know, from that gay movie—he OD'd there once."

Reena wrinkles an eyebrow. "I think you're thinking of the Viper Room."

"Not the Alley Cat?"

"The *Back Alley*!" I say, kind of freaking out.

Jonas is not fazed. "Yossi, man," he says, drumming out a rhythm on the back of my seat, inciting increasingly creative and elaborate murderous thoughts in me, "you're going to be pimping it to synagogue on Shabbos from now on, huh? No more flying coach."

"I'm shomer Shabbos," Yossi says simply. "I don't drive."

"Right, right," Jonas agrees quickly. "Well, you know—then wherever else you go. You'll be a *pimp*."

Jonas might be on to something, if it weren't for two basic facts.

One: I'm guessing Yossi doesn't go to too many places other than synagogue or Gittleman to begin with. Besides the Back Alley, randomly, that is.

Two: "Yossi hardly strikes me as the pimp type."

Saying this out loud makes me laugh, which makes me guffaw, and finally, collapse into a clunky outright snort. Yossi's not a pimp.

And, seriously? Thank God for that.

• • •

That actor from that gay movie may not have OD'd here, but somewhere, sometime, someone definitely did. This place has just too many shady corners with suspiciously sticky, powdery surfaces. It smells like a mixture of industrial bleach, sweat, and aged vomit. And it totally beats new car smell. It's punk rock and gritty and makes me a little bit queasy.

I love it. I love the Back Alley.

I'm pressed against the doorway leading from the bar to the main stage, just soaking it all in the way Jonas did in Yossi's Jeep. Love and Sprockets owns the rickety little joint; the lead singer grips at his mic and stomps up and down, the veins in his stringy arms pulsing and bulging, and his sweat-soaked emo hair flicking droplets across the stage. The music is some kind of hybrid of White Stripes stripped-down guitar riffs blended with Postal Service synthesized loops. It's crazy. It's *genius.* I can feel the indie-cred seeping into my bones, oozing from the splintery walls of this place and creeping down to the belly of my soul.

I'm not the only one. Somehow, even though we're kind of out of our element, all of the members of the Tribe are totally into this place, in our way.

The minute we got here, Reena let the beefy bouncer at the door stamp the back of her hand as under twenty-one— not even pretending to be in possession of ID—then ran off to press her way to the front of the stage. I can barely make her out now, except for the tips of her tufted little ponytail. The no-frills clips pinned at her temples glimmer when the flickery glow of the main room's bare bulbs hit them right in their shiny plastic grooved edges. She's like a pop art installation. It's funny—she's tiny, but she takes up so much space. I don't get how that works.

Yossi surveys the merch table, fingering limited-edition singles and silk-screened tees. He bobs his head, though, so I know that he's absorbing at least some of the music, even if it's a peripheral kind of thing for him. He's our wheels. Our *pimp.*

Jonas has gone AWOL, which further proves my theory that he's totally doing his own thing, whatever that entails. I have a sinking suspicion it includes regaling naïve underclass(wo)men with tales of dashing and daring hardcoreitude.

I can just see it: he's leaning up, pressing his mouth-breathing lips to their delicate, studded pink earlobes and quoting select favorites of his lyrical children, *man*; he's letting them bathe in *eau du* new car. He's shrewdly calculating, figuring a plan for sneaking backstage and wreaking real rock-star havoc, chair-smashing and beer-guzzling straight from the tap.

In my fantasy, Jonas is a lot like a young Ozzy Osbourne, oddly. Or one of the members of ZZ Top, *sans* freaky beard.

My fantasy, mixed with the pulsing laser light show I'm getting of Reena in the pit and the stench of one hundred and twenty straight-waisted, blunt-banged, skinny-jeaned hipsters swaying with calculated nonchalance, is making me dizzy.

I need air. Air, or a pair of newer, skinnier jeans.

Air is easier to come by right now, so air it is. I focus on the EXIT sign at the front of the building and wander toward it with mechanical deliberation.

I don't get very far, though, before I feel a thick hand clutching eagerly at my shoulder.

"Wanna beer?" Jonas asks me, eyes glittering.

"Wha-how—" I start, then realize I really don't give a crap about the "how." "Yeah, sure."

He pulls me into a darkened ante room, smiling at a group of pale girls with long dark hair who recline languidly on sofas that look scavenged from a real back alley somewhere.

"Alexis, Perry, Maneesha"—he nods at each of them as he introduces them; they wave wanly toward me—"this is Ari. He's with the Tribe." He winks.

I'm with the Tribe. I'm *in* the Tribe. I'm certainly not the one person solely responsible for the Tribe's existence. Nope. Not me.

"Maneesha's sister's boyfriend bought some beers for us." He presses a bottle, cool and damp with perspiration, into my palm. Amstel Light. How punk rock. "'Cause I was telling her about us." A beefy redheaded guy scowls at us. I think he's Maneesha's sister's boyfriend. He looks a little bit put out by the whole scene. I hope Jonas paid him for the beer.

Maneesha seems much more impressed by us herself. No doubt Jonas was giving her the hard sell. Frankly, it sounds like maybe he wasn't exactly telling her the whole story—like, in his version, he's the rock god who brought us all together in musical union. But okay, I can forgive a lot of things—and in particular, being relegated to Jonas' wingman, as usual—if there's beer involved. Even if it is girl beer.

"Where'd you get the girl beer?" Reena wanders over, winded and flushed from being slammed up against the stage. She's got Yossi in tow. He's brandishing a long-sleeved Love and Sprockets tee shirt that will definitely be an upgrade to his usual wardrobe.

"Maneesha's sister's ..." I begin, then realize that she doesn't really care, and it doesn't really matter.

She grabs the bottle playfully out of my hand and takes a healthy swig. "We're sharing," she says. She takes another gulp, then gives Maneesha and Co. a thorough once-over. Is she thinking the same thing I'm thinking?

"Jonas is pretty cute when he wants to be, right?" she asks the girls, eyes sparkling. "Don't worry, he knows it. That's why he's our frontman."

Suddenly I want to barf. Has Reena been drinking the Kool-Aid? I guess that's the thing about infectious charm. You never see it coming, always underestimate its capacity.

Jonas grins, not at all bashful, and pushes another beer at Yossi, who waves it off.

"Don't drink."

Jonas cackles maniacally. Yossi is a regular Dane Cook.

If Dane Cook were kosher. Or Jewish. Or if Yossi were even remotely cool. "Of course you don't, man. *F^&*.*"

A flicker of disgust passes across Reena's face, the corners of her mouth going flat in either direction. Seriously—is she thinking what I'm thinking?

"It's hip to be square," she says limply. "Don't you know?"

"Yeah." Jonas laughs again, sniffling a little this time around the carbonation in his beer. "Yossi is the king of cool. *Not.*"

Yossi's face has gone impassive and I'm feeling that sense of suffocation again. Reena looks like she wants to poke Jonas in the eyeball with one of her hair clips. Now I'm certain she's thinking what I'm thinking. God bless her.

Maneesha picks up on the tension in the air, not that that makes her a genius at reading a room or anything. She twirls a strand of greasy black hair around a long, skinny, unpolished fingernail. "So, Tribe," she begins, her voice doing that singsongy up-talk thing that drives me nuts (in the bad way), unless of course it's Sari Horowitz doing the up-talking. "Yossi's the drums, and Reena's backup vocals." Like she's going to be quizzed on this later. "And Jonas is the frontman. Lead vocals. Lead guitar."

A bowling ball slams me in the gut. *I'm* lead guitar. *I'm* the leader of the band, whether Jonas has the charm or not. I'm the one who brought us all together, and I'm the one who had the brilliant plan to put Jonas on bass, like all quasi-incompetent but intensely self-important musicians throughout history.

My idea. My band. My ticket to high school notoriety. Me, me, me.

I'm having a temper tantrum on the inside.

Maneesha squints at me, flipping her curtain of hair over one shoulder. "So, Ari," she asks, causing a cold fist to squeeze at my lower intestines. The likelihood that she is about to say something that's going to send me completely over the edge is high. Like, 98.8 percent high.

"I don't get it. What's your whole connection to the Tribe? Like, what do you do?" she asks, driving that fist in my stomach up through my throat until I feel like I'm choking on it.

My connection to the Tribe. Like, what do I do?

I want to toss my beer bottle at the nearest wall. Young Ozzy Osbourne, indeed.

Maybe I'm not even sure what I do, anymore. I seem to spend a good chunk of my time being extremely pissed off at Jonas. But that's not, like, a thing. A contribution. A role to play.

Even if it is pretty punk rock. And not in the ZZ Top kind of way.

twelve

Dude, you were kind of a dick to Maneesha."

I shove a French fry into my mouth and shrug, ignoring Jonas' accusing stare.

The Forum diner on Northfield Ave. is a major Gittleman hangout. For the kids who don't slave over their homework, or hole up on their bed pretending to write pseudo-intellectual indie-rock songs every night, that is. Meaning that this is one of the rare occasions that I've been here past 5:00 PM.

It looks completely different at 1:13 in the morning. For starters, chicks with straight-ironed hair and velour track suits giggle and whisper and pretend to eat things like chicken fingers, which would never happen in the pre-dinner hours. In the pre-dinner hours it's strictly salad, all the way. Dressing on the side.

(Sari's an "on the side" type. It's really annoying.)

More than that, the lighting is all off—weird, pallid, and yellowish, well-matched to the waxy complexions of the sunken-cheeked wait staff. It feels like we've stumbled into an alternative universe of night people, mole-folk who haven't seen sunlight in eons. It's exotic and thrilling. Diner of the damned. And damn cool.

Also, my French fries are killer. And are providing me a much-needed distraction from my overwhelming urge to lunge across the table and rip off Jonas' rockabilly-wannabe sideburns.

Sideburns. He has *sideburns,* now.

"Seriously, dude. What's your deal?"

• • •

I look up from my plate. My *deal* is that Jonas was starving after the Love and Sprockets show and insisted that we stop by the Forum for "munchies" (a term that disgusts me almost as much as "on the side"), and that despite the fact that it is currently requiring all of my energy not to smash Jonas in the face with the heel of my palm, Yossi is my ride. Damn cool diner or no, I don't want to be here. But I have no way of being anywhere else.

I pick up my fork and fiddle with it, considering my reply. "It's—"

"Jonas," Reena cuts in, shooting me a nervous look from over the table. She is nestled against the wall and has been sneaking glances at the colorful but sadly stocked jukebox that graces our booth. "Since when are you lead guitar?"

Well-said. I put my fork down and wait on his reply.

He shifts in his seat. Does he look uncomfortable? Nah, not Jonas.

"Whatever," he smugs. "I was just thinking, you know, that it's good to change things up. So people don't get stale and stuff. No big deal, for f^&*'s sake."

No big deal. I slam my palms against the table. My cup of coffee jitters, sloshing watery brown liquid over its edge into a pool on its saucer. I feel a little bit embarrassed. But still.

"Dude," I say, practically snarling, "you don't, like, make a decision like that without talking to people first. You don't even *think* about it." And since when has Jonas given *any* thought to anything to do with the Tribe without my prompting, anyway?

My eyes feel hot and prickly, to my surprise, which means I may or may not be about to cry. I haven't cried since Simchat Torah four years ago, when I was high on candy apples and accidentally slammed my bedroom window down on my right middle and ring fingers. I still have the scars. And it was pathetic then. Crying: not an option.

"God, do you think you might be overreacting?" Jonas says, his voice now doing the girly up-talk. He's singsongy just to show me how seriously he *doesn't* take me. Beautiful.

Yossi clears his throat. "You shouldn't take the Lord's name in vain."

Now we all turn to stare at him, our bloodlust and crackling tension temporarily shelved.

"What the *f^&**, man?" Jonas arches an eyebrow in utter disbelief.

Yossi blinks, gathering himself, and then seems to tap into some inner reserve. He breathes sharply. "I mean it," he says, clearly meaning it. "I can't stand that. So quit it. Or, at least, quit it around me."

Jonas looks completely taken aback. Gobsmacked. Like if you'd told him that Fallout Boy had just split up or something. He runs his fingers through his hair, sending those carefully cultivated sideburns in every direction. He picks up his glass of water and gulps greedily, replacing it sloppily back onto the table, just adjacent to the wet ring from where it rested moments before.

"Whatever," he says finally.

"It doesn't matter," I say angrily. I mean the Jonas thing, not the Yossi Up-With-the-Holy-One thing. Even though it totally does matter.

"It totally does matter," Reena protests. "I mean, the whole band was your idea."

Thank you.

"And anyway, there was a reason you gave Jonas bass. Bass is like, the mysterious, cool, indie part. He should be *flattered.*" She pivots on her elbows to look Jonas squarely in the eyes. "You should be flattered. He could have kept bass for himself."

Jonas snorts. "He can't even play bass."

"Seriously?" Reena is dubious. "Let's talk about how rad your skills were, how excellent you were at bass, when Ari first approached you." Two little splotches of pink stand out on her cheeks against her porcelain skin. She's furious. It's shocking.

It's *cute.*

"Thank you," I say, turning to her. "I guess that's true." I guess.

Jonas shakes his head. I can tell he's not convinced, but he can definitely sense dissension in the ranks. He's out of Kool-Aid, outnumbered.

"Fine." He swigs at his water again. "It doesn't matter."

"Reena's right. It matters. We need to figure it out for sure," Yossi says. This is the second most decisive thing Yossi has ever said to us, coming directly after asking Jonas not to take the Lord's name in vain. It's a big night for him.

"Yeah, I guess," I say.

"No," Yossi insists. "I mean that we *have* to figure out, for sure, before next Saturday."

"Dude, what the f^&* is next Saturday?" Jonas asks.

He laughs a short, bitter chuckle. "You want us to do Havdalah together as a band?"

Havdalah is the ceremony that officially separates the Sabbath from the regular old unholy week. Candles, wine, religion … not exactly punk rock.

"There's a battle of the bands," Yossi mumbles. "I thought we could enter."

"What?" Now I'm the one up on my elbows and looking astonished. That Yossi would know about a battle of the bands, but I wouldn't, is unfathomable. Inexcusable.

The pink from Reena's cheeks spreads slowly across her face, like a paintbrush dipped in water in between color changes. She's a palate of emotion, and for a moment, I'm in a trance.

Then she snaps out of it, and I do, too.

"Where did you hear about a battle of the bands?" She crosses her arms across her chest, then uncrosses them and dives over the table to snag one of my French fries, stuffing it in her mouth and chewing thoughtfully. "Needs mayo," she offers after a contemplative beat.

The difference between ketchup and mayo on fries is like the difference between Nico and Neko. I'm willing to forgive it or even, possibly, partake in some open-mindedness if the waiter ever wanders by again. If all of the plate-slamming and dramatic gasping going on at our table hasn't piqued his attention, then I don't know what will.

"Tonight," Yossi offers. "I heard about it tonight."

That's more of a *when* than a *where* but since it's also

helpful information, I can work with it. "At the *Back Alley*?" My voice almost cracks and I wince, but I can't hide my incredulousness.

"Yeah, I was talking to the bouncer."

Jonas' jaw drops open. "That's where you disappeared to, man?" He laughs. "That's f^&*ing awesome."

"He was a really nice guy," Yossi says. "He's an expert on Spinoza."

Spinoza was an Enlightenment philosopher. No one under the age of eighty should be an expert on Spinoza. Most especially not huge, tattooed, hard-core bouncers at indie rock clubs. Not at all.

"How did that even come up?" Reena asks. Her eyes are tiny slits of bafflement.

"I don't know. But he is. And he has a study group that meets at his apartment once a month. Somewhere downtown. Near Katz's deli, he says. Which I know isn't kosher, but Leonard says there are other places nearby that are. Leonard. That's his name."

Reena explodes. Her laugh is infectious. "So you're going to join a Spinoza study group with *Leonard*, the scholarly bouncer from the Back Alley, and eat kosher deli with him on a semi-regular basis?"

"I guess so," Yossi says, completely deadpan, completely not getting why our minds are all so completely blown. "But anyway. They're having a battle of the bands on Saturday, and one of the bands that was scheduled to compete dropped out at the last minute. So he said that if we want it, the gig's ours. We just have to call tomorrow when the guy who does the scheduling is in. Leonard will put in a good word for us."

Do we want it? Of course we want it. It's the one thing we'll all be able to agree on, the whole night.

"F^&* yeah, we want it," Jonas enthuses, and for the first time in what feels like a century, I want to slap him on the back in a friendly, all-for-one-and-one-for-all sort of way, rather than a "Choke on it, butthead" sort of way.

"We're gonna have to play something original," I say, slapping my trusty notebook down on the table. "No covers. Something killer."

"Yeah, I mean, our songs are, like, our children, *man,*" Reena chimes in, grinning in a way that exposes her tiny overbite.

She makes to grab for my fries again, but instead snatches my notebook away. I sit up, then lean back against the booth again. Suave.

"You've been dragging this thing around everywhere since we first got the band together," she says. "You have to have *something* useful in here." She flips through the pages.

"That's ... um, private," I mumble, quietly enough that when she ignores me I can sort of pretend it's because she didn't hear me right.

Her eyes light up on one of my drawings. I can tell the moment she realizes what they are—that is to say, sketches, rather than song lyrics—because her mouth makes a perfect little "o" shape and her eyebrows knit together. My face feels hot and I wonder if she's looking at one that has her in it.

Oh God.

She coughs delicately and slides the notebook back toward me, avoiding the smeary water ring moat that Jonas has engineered.

"Well," she says. "I'm sure we can come up with something between now and then."

• • •

It's not until much later, when I'm home, in bed, idly doodling and replaying the evening in my mind, that I realize: the Battle of the Bands is scheduled for the Saturday night before the last week of school.

Otherwise known as the night before the SATs.

We are so totally screwed.

INSIDE: THE PEE SMELL IN ROOM 215. EXPERTS WEIGH IN ON WHERE IT MAY BE COMING FROM.

HAS TRIBE GONE TRAIF?

THE GITTLEMAN Star

ARI: "I CAN'T CONTROL MY BAND."

JONAS: RUNNING FOR CLASS PRESIDENT?!

THE CANDIDATE'S CONTRAVERSIAL STANCE ON #2 PENCILS: "THEY F^&*ING SUCK!"

ANOTHER DETENTION!!!
REENA: "I'M NOT SORRY."

INSIDE SOURCES TALK ABOUT HER GYM-CUTTING MARATHON AND WHY HER OUTRAGEOUS ANTICS AREN'T LIKELY TO STOP.

YOSSI: CAUGHT DRIVING ON SHABBOS!

WITH PORK CHOP IN HAND!!

PLUS: EIGHTH GRADE OVERNIGHT TO WASHINGTON DC A SUCCESS!

THIS YEAR NO STUDENTS LEFT BEHIND IN NATION'S CAPITOL.

ARI'S SHOCKING STATEMENT!
AT THIS POINT, I THINK IT'S FAIR TO SAY THAT WE'RE MORE POPULAR THAN MOSES. I MEAN, HE **DID** LAY THE GROUND-WORK BUT I THINK WEVE TAKEN THINGS IN A WHOLE NEW DIRECTION.
IS THAT WHY YOU'VE TAKEN TO CARRYING AROUND THAT STAFF?
IT WAS A FACTOR.
HIPSTER COWBOY

JONAS' UNRELENTING VANITY!
HOW MANY TIMES CAN I SAY IT? NO PICTURES, GUYS! MY SKIN IS VERY SENSITIVE TO THE PHOSPHORESCENCE!
SO DUDE, YOU ARE OR ARE NOT IN LINE FOR PIZZA DAY?

REENA'S DOWNWARD SPIRAL!
WHAT'S UP CHOIR BIZNATCHES? SO, ARE WE GOING TO SING, OR ARE WE GOING TO SIT HERE LOOKING LIKE BIZNATCHES?
GOOD GOD, HOW MANY VENTI-ICED-VANILLA-SOY LATTES DID SHE HAVE TODAY?
GET BENT FINKLESTIEN I HAVE A PRESCRIPTION!

YOSSI'S BOLD DENIALS!
WYNONA WHO? ARE YOU TALKING ABOUT THAT FRESH-MAN WHO ALWAYS STARES AT ME DURING PRAYERS? WELL, WE CANT EVEN BRING FRESHMEN TO THE PROM SO I'M AFRAID THAT SOMEONE'S MISTAKEN.

thirteen

Wandering Jews

Any good little Gittle-man knows that you haven't done your time as a member of the tribe until you've been on an Exodus of sorts—which means it's completely par for the course that the Tribe is on the move.

The rumors are true, folks—see your favorite kosher boys (plus one girl, of course) rocking out at the Lower East Side's Back Alley annual Battle of the Bands. This Saturday night, at—you guessed it—the Back Alley, LES.

Come for the school spirit. Stay for the debut of the Tribe's first original song. We're gonna need way more than a minyan to rock the house. Seriously, folks—the SATs will be there again next year for retesting. We promise.

"I saw the article about your show," Sari whispers to me.

From the front of the classroom, Elkin glances at us. Sari's whisper is not much quieter than her regular speaking voice.

I guess when you're that cute, you feel like everyone deserves to hear what you have to say. I am, empirically speaking, less cute, and so I just shrug. Elkin likes me. No sense in doing anything to change that fact.

But, wait. "It's not really a show," I correct her, taking advantage of the need to lean in close so that she can hear me. She smells like gum again—this time watermelon flavor. Typically I'm not a fan of the fruit—too much water, not enough melon—but Sari just has this *effect* on me. "It's a contest, you know? A competition."

She taps her fingers against the surface of her desk. I don't think she's very impressed with this subtle distinction. "Well, Jonas said he's working on a new song."

Of course he did.

"We're all working." Mostly. If by "all working" you mean, "getting together at the Forum after dinner every night to chew on the tips of our pencils and stare blankly into space through our thinly-veiled simmering resentments."

"Well, I can't wait." Sari smiles. "Jonas is so good. And you are, too," she adds generously, smoothing out her magenta wool skirt underneath her.

Neither statements are true, really, but I'll take them.

"The final," Elkin announces, slightly louder and with more urgency than his general monotone usually conveys, "will be two weeks from today." He glares at Sari and me, then scribbles a date on the blackboard. I swear he squeaks the chalk on purpose. My teeth curl back in my gums.

"Oh God," Sari sighs, and for a minute I want to tell her not to take the Lord's name in vain. "I'm so going to fail."

"Nah," I say, elbowing her in the side. She has a nice side. "I'm tutoring you, remember?"

"But you're so busy these days," she says, pouting at me.

"It's fine." It's so much more than fine.

"God, Ari," she says again, which again makes me think of Yossi and what he would have to say about all of this wanton blasphemy, "between Calc and the Battle of the Bands, I'm going to be, like, all over you."

Yeah, I think. *I hope so.*

• • •

Sari all over me would be more than enough, you know? Like, I could die happy knowing that she's suddenly completely obsessed with all of my comings and goings. But the truth is, she may be the Tribe's biggest fan, but she's not the only fan by a long shot. *Everyone's* seen the piece in the *Gittleman Star*. And *everyone* that I talk to is planning to hit the Back Alley on Saturday night. Our MySpace page has totally exploded and it's getting so the comments run for lines and lines and lines.

I had no idea people were so cavalier about the SATs. I should really get their parents to talk to my parents.

Also—and this is a complete Hanukkah miracle—I think we've found some inspiration. Yossi pounded out a rhythm the other day and the words just flowed from there. We're almost ready. We may not sweep the Battle of the Bands, but we're not going to completely humiliate ourselves, either. So that's something.

That's actually a lot.

• • •

I don't know why they call it "reading comprehension." Seriously, it should definitely be called "boredom instigation," since if we're going to be all open and frank, that's what these passages do. The only way to keep from face-planting straight down into my SAT-prep book while I mindlessly scan excerpt after excerpt is to blast some Offspring while I "study." *Offspring.* Is this really what I've been reduced to? Strum-*strum,* strum *strum,* strum-*strum.* Faux-punk is almost as boring as reading comprehension, actually.

The music is loud enough that I almost don't hear the knock at my bedroom door. Curious. My parents are, as usual, not home from work yet. And Ben, of course, doesn't knock. But there it is again—tentative, but upbeat.

I lower the volume on my iPod speakers. "Come in."

"Offspring?" Reena cocks an eyebrow at me. "Oh, Ari. I would have expected Offspring from Jonas. But you? You're better than that."

I laugh, completely disarmed despite the fact that this may be the very first time a member of the opposite sex has been in my bedroom, not counting cousin Frieda at Passover seder five years ago.

Reena is way different from cousin Frieda.

And she's *here.*

Why is she here?

"*Kafka on the Shore*?" She darts greedily toward my bedside table.

Shoot. Of course she'd notice that first. I should have put it somewhere less conspicuous. But how was I to know that Reena Gluck would suddenly appear, materialize seemingly from thin air, a vision of brunette deadpan irony, right in my bedroom doorway? Duh.

"I thought you were reading *Kafka* Kafka, not Murakami Kafka." She picks up the book and flips through it. "You haven't gotten very far."

To be honest, I got stuck around chapter four and haven't had the energy to pick it up since then. It's pretty dense. But I don't want her thinking I'm a moron or otherwise mentally inferior.

"I've been busy," I say. "Hey, how'd you get in here, anyway?"

"Through the challenging and courageous act of ringing the doorbell," she informs me, sinking into the khaki-colored armchair that's been in my room since I was four. Suddenly, the chair seems totally immature and stupid. It was given to my parents as a present when I was born, and really isn't grown-person sized. Still, Reena fits into its seat neatly, snug and comfortable-looking. "Your brother let me in. Are your parents going to freak about you having a girl in your room while they're out? I mean, mine wouldn't, but you never know." She smiles crookedly.

I've just been wondering the very same thing, but I cover. "They don't care. I mean, they don't have a rule against it or anything." Probably because, like me, they didn't ever anticipate a girl-in-room-alone scenario presenting itself anytime before I hit thirty. But still.

"Cool. Well, Yossi drove me over. He'll come get me in a little bit."

"Cool," I agree, not sure what to do—not with myself, not with Reena—now that I'm actually in a girl-in-room-alone scenario fully fourteen years earlier than expected.

"So, Saturday is the Battle of the Bands," she says, clasping her hands in her lap and swinging her legs forward and back. "You think we're ready?"

"Pretty ready," I say. As ready as we're going to be. But we've got a new song, and it's a good one. Basic enough that we won't screw it up, but with enough room to impress the judges. We've practiced every night this week. I think having the Battle to look forward to has given us the sack to deal with each other and not get on each other's nerves so much. For a little while, that is. For now.

"What do you think?" I ask.

"Yeah, yeah," she says, waving her hand. "But, I came over here ... "

She trails off, looking slightly embarrassed. I don't think I've ever seen Reena look embarrassed before. It's totally adorable. Even her ears blush, sort of. "Well."

She bends over her messenger bag and roots around in it for a while, exposing the underside of her neck to me. It's blushing, too, like her ears. How can one person blush so much?

"Here." She stands up and crosses toward me, dropping a small packet of shiny papers and cards and stuff on my desk that spill off into a frenetic fan.

I sift through it all, my eyes catching on colorful words and bold phrases. "This is ... a New Jersey transit schedule. And a MetroCard for the Manhattan subway. And ... a map of West Village?"

"Greenwich Village, really," Reena says. "NYU."

I'm so confused. "NYU?"

I swear, even her eyelashes are flaming red right now. "It's just ... I know that your parents want you to apply to Brandeis. But that you don't want to go there."

She knows this? Did we talk about it? I can't recall, but I guess we must have. And even still, if we did—I can't believe she remembers all that, anyway, or that she's given it any more thought.

"So, well… NYU has a really good visual arts program."

"Visual arts?" If she didn't think I was mentally inferior before, she's going to start having some doubts pretty freaking soon. I sound like an idiot, even to my own ears.

"Like, um, design, and animation, and, you know…" She clears her throat and curls back up in the shrunken armchair, looking extremely small and vulnerable from across the room. "Like your drawings."

She swallows, then nods to herself, seeming to gather some resolve, and looks directly at me. "They're really good."

"I mean…" I shrug. "They're fine."

"They're *really good*," she repeats. "And anyway… uh, NYU has a lot of Jewish students. They've got a Hillel center, and it's New York, so, you know, maybe it wouldn't be too hard to convince your parents to at least let you apply."

I have to admit, I'm really curious. I've spent so much time not-wanting to go to Brandeis that I haven't bothered to come up with any alternatives. I have no idea where I want to go.

And I have *no* idea why Reena has given this more thought than I have. But obviously she has.

"They have a gallery. Where students post their artwork. And an information center. And it's open on weekends."

"Yeah?" I'm finally picking up on where she may be going with this.

"You can even take a tour and stuff. I've got maps of the campus, too, on my computer."

She looks embarrassed for a minute, like maybe she's given too much away. Then she looks defiant. "So do you want to go?"

"To NYU?"

She nods.

"I guess I ... don't know. I need to do some research."

She shakes her head, clearly losing patience with me. "Not, like, um, next year for college. For *now.* For Saturday. We could take a tour. Check it out."

For now. For Saturday. For real.

That sounds awesome.

Seeing my expression and getting it, she warms to her pitch. "Yossi can't drive us 'cause it's Shabbos, but we can take a cab to the train station. It's really easy to get down to NYU from Penn Station on the subway."

"You've done it before?" I'm doubtful.

She flushes, answering my question for me. "There's a map and stuff online. It's the red line. Or one of the orange ones."

This response isn't all that comforting, and yet, strangely, I'm not particularly concerned. We'll take the red line, or one of the orange ones, and we'll get lost, or we won't. Either way, the whole thing sounds like a perfectly cool way to kill a Saturday afternoon. But what about—

"The equipment? For the gig?"

"Yossi and Jonas can handle it."

"Jonas is going to be pissed."

"No, he won't. He'll be too geared up for the battle to really care. And anyway, I already talked to Yossi about it, and he said he doesn't mind loading up the van himself. So we're covered, even if Jonas does decide to freak."

It must be said: the girl's thought of everything.

For *me.* She's thought of everything for *me.*

Bizarre.

"You're in, then. We're gonna do it. You don't have a choice." She smirks at me. "I'll get the cab to come around two on Saturday. That way we have plenty of time to get lost on the campus, and still get down to the Lower East Side in time for the show."

"Sure," I say. There doesn't seem to be much more to add. Like I say, she's thought of *everything*. It's pretty handy.

She pushes herself up and out of the chair, yawning as she gets to her feet. "Cool. I'll call Yossi and have him come get me. But yeah ... " She gestures at my desk and all of the stuff she brought over. "Surprise."

"Surprise," I agree. I shift in my seat, wanting to get up and walk her to the front door, but then suddenly feel all awkward about it and instead stay firmly rooted, fixed at my desk. Rude, but ... rooted. Fixed. *Trans*fixed.

"Don't worry," she says, meaning the getting-up thing (or the *not* getting-up thing, I guess). "I've got it. So Saturday."

I nod. "It's a date."

She doesn't say anything, just turns and leaves. I hear her shuffle down the stairs. Her bowling shoes make scuffing sounds against the hardwood floors. I idly hope she isn't leaving any marks. And then as her footsteps grow fainter, it hits me—what I've said.

"It's a date."

A *date.*

And now I have to wonder if it is, or if that's just some stupid thing that people say, that *I* said, or what. Or if it is in fact a date, if that's good or bad. As I think I've mentioned, I've never been on a date before. Not a real one, anyway. So I'm not entirely sure what it even entails.

I'm totally confused. And totally overwhelmed. And totally looking forward to Saturday.

fourteen

Saturday.

8:42 AM: Peel eyes open. Feels not unlike sandpaper. Glance at clock. Oh-my-jeez. Back to sleep.

8:57 AM: Today's my field trip with Reena. To NYU.

9:03 AM: Tonight's the *gig.*

9:14 AM: I have no idea what to wear. Need to be more alterna than Abercrombie.

9:20 AM: Probably not very punk-rock for a guy to be worried about what to wear.

9:31 AM: Four hours, twenty-nine minutes until the cab comes.

With Reena.

For our "date."

9:55 AM: Screw it. I'm up.

• • •

I'm not the only one up with the garbage trucks (the suburban alternative to being up with the chickens). When I stumble out of my bedroom and toward the kitchen in search of a Cap'n-Crunch fix, I nearly trip over Ben, who has somehow taken over the den, turning it into his own private, personal arcade.

"You're awake," he observes.

"You're brilliant."

"I know," he shrugs.

"I was kidding."

"I wasn't." He twists away from the television set, contorting his body impossibly. "Wanna play Wii?"

Nyet, nein, non. I have way too much on my rock-star mind for that right now.

"Can't," I say, being deliberately vague. "Too bad, Benny."

"Right." He glances at the digital clock flashing on the TV cable box. "Your cab is coming in, like, four hours."

He rolls his eyes while I leap around the couch and crouch next to him on the shaggy carpeting, sliding into what I hope—but doubt—is a casual seated position.

"Wha—what are you talking about?"

Very smooth.

"At two, right? To go to the—"

"Shh!" I clap my hand over his mouth before he can give me away. "How do you know about that?"

He fixes me with a *duh* look.

"You were listening at my door?" I shove him, realizing. "Dick." I pull the Wii controls out of his hands, as solemn as I can possibly be. "Listen. You can't tell Mom and Dad."

He sticks his tongue out at me. Very mature. "Or?"

"I'll kill you."

"No, you won't."

He's probably right. I'm kind of wussy and non-violent that way. But still.

"I'll be really pissed. I'll *never* play Wii with you. Or stick up for you at school. Or help you out if you get teachers that I had. Even though I saved *all* of my tests." This much, at least, I can promise.

"You don't play Wii with me anyway. You're graduating high school soon. And my grades are fine." Ben ticks off each of his respective points on his pudgy little fingers one by one, smirking deeply all the while.

I wish he'd smirk so wide he'd swallow his whole face.

"Come on, Ben," I say, at a loss. "Don't be a jackass."

"Well, maybe there's *one* way that you could keep me from telling," he says, his eyes glinting with intent.

I sigh. "Yes?"

Every single feature on his face spills over with self-satisfaction. "You could take me with you. To the city. To NYU. And to your show."

• • •

When the cab comes, I tell my parents that it's Jonas, picking me up for the night. I'm staying at his house while Ben has a "sleepover" at Matt Sherman's. I had to swear on pain of summer school that Jonas and I would be flashcarding the night away, that I'd get at least seven and a half hours of sleep, eat a balanced breakfast (protein, carbs, and some form of plant life), and arrive at the SAT testing site at least twenty minutes early Sunday morning, but Mom believed me when I told her that Jonas needed me for last-minute cramming.

Truth is, Jonas probably *does* need me for last-minute cramming. But it's not likely to happen tonight.

Reena's cab is a Town Car, sleek and upscale, and I'm glad that my parents didn't bother to peek out the window when they heard the horn honk.

"Welcome to my funeral procession of one," she says dryly as Ben and I slide into the back seat with her.

"And here I thought you were on your way to the Oscars," I say, suddenly feeling the tension go out of my body and finding, at the same time, that I'm really into going to the city with Reena.

To Ben she asks, "Where are we dropping you?"

"I'm coming with you," he smugs.

A quick nod of my head confirms the unfortunate truth. But if Reena is daunted, she doesn't let it show. "Right on," she says. "Cool." She loops her elbow through his own and he's completely smitten.

I think I know the feeling.

• • •

NYU is sprawling, unstructured, overwhelming. Students stroll by, some lazily, some looking like they're on the verge of a comprehensive nervous breakdown, some looking like they might not be students but supermodels, Hollywood B-listers between films or actual fledgling rock stars. It's a sea of carefully-cultivated facial hair, messy buns, track pants, and enormous, oversized to-go cups of coffee.

It's amazing.

"Those are dorms," Reena says, waving her hand in the general direction of a narrow side street off of Washington Square Park. "Or"—she squints at her campus map—"possibly the computer lab. Or the health center."

"Is that even a map of NYU?" I ask, suddenly suspicious. I grab at the unwieldy folds of paper and she ducks away from me, giggling. I didn't know girls like Reena giggled. A dimple forms on her lower left cheek and her eyes twinkle.

"What's that?" Ben asks, pointing.

I look over at where he indicates. "The Arc de Triomphe."

"The Arc de Triomphe is in Paris," he argues, prompting me to marvel at what, exactly, he's learning in sixth grade social studies. I thought European studies came later. But then, I guess we always knew he was a child prodigy.

"This one," I say calmly, "is here." I roll my eyes over his head at Reena, causing her to giggle again. I find that I like being able to make her giggle.

"So should we make a plan or something?" Reena

asks, her breath puffing out little clouds into the cold air. "'Cause it's way too cold to be wandering aimlessly."

I nod. "But I don't think it's worth it to try to find a dorm. You need student ID to be able to get in one, or a tour guide. Like, a real NYU one."

"There's a coffee place in the student union," she says. "That could be fun. You could pretend like you're an artsy NYU student. You're dressed for it, anyway." She means because my hair's doing that flippy emo thing under my knit cap. It's on purpose for the show. But I'm a little embarrassed to have her point it out, even though I sort of wanted her to notice.

"Shut up," I say. But I'm smiling.

• • •

Ben orders a hot chocolate with whipped cream, and Reena gets a latte that she lets me pay for. I mean, I think that's just the polite thing to do, especially since she came up with the whole idea of today in the first place. Anyway, I get a black coffee because it seems the most hardcore, but after one sip I dump about half of the sugar canister into my mug, wincing. *So* punk rock. But not.

"So what do you think?" Reena asks me, as we settle ourselves at a small table right in the window. There's kind of a draft, but I don't care. I'm in a people-watching trance, and I can tell that Reena is, too. For his part, Ben is clearly just star-struck to be spending the afternoon with us. Yeah, he's a pain, but I still kind of dig on it.

"It's . . . amazing," I say after a minute. "Kind of confusing, like the way everything is all over the place, but I guess that's just the city."

"Yeah, I mean, there isn't really a campus, but there's always something going on. I just think—like, think about the people you'd meet here. What sort of stuff you could do, on your own for four years."

"I could keep on top of the whole music scene," I muse.

Reena tilts her head at me. "Come on."

"What?" I sip my coffee, grimacing again. Really, really not hardcore. I dump another small pile of sugar into the mug, creating a thick sludge.

"The music scene? Ari, I seriously hope you mean going to shows, not playing them."

"Why not?" I ask, defensive. "It could happen." It sounds a little bit like she's insulting my sweet licks, and I bristle.

"Yeah," she says shortly, obviously meaning "no." She folds her hands on the table in front of her. Ben's eyes dart from my face to hers like he's watching a tennis match.

"I don't get it," she continues, finally.

"What?"

"Why music is so important to you. I mean," she goes on, very quickly all of a sudden, "I get that *music* is important, but I just don't see why you're so hung up on the whole band thing."

Her eyes are glassy and bright, and she's taking big

gulps of breath between her sentences. "The Tribe is fine, but we're not, like, gonna be the next Nirvana or anything. And I'm not sure why you're so desperate for us to be." She looks down.

"I'm not desperate." I'm *not* desperate. Really.

I am, however, sort of edgy.

"You're really talented," she says, "at *art*."

And then she does the weirdest thing. She, like, reaches across the table toward my hand. But as the tips of her goth-red nails approach, something in her snaps, like she realizes that she's maybe—what? Holding my hand? Trying to?

Never mind. Whatever it was, the moment is gone. She straightens up in her seat and keeps talking, not quite meeting my gaze.

"Really talented. At drawing. Like, *really* talented. I mean, if you're searching for some sort of... *thing*... I kind of feel like—that's it. It's a thing. And it's a good thing."

"But being in a band is *cool*," Ben offers.

The kid's right. Not only that, but he's boiled the whole thing down to its purest form.

Reena shrugs. "So's art. Honestly."

"But not in that rocker way," Ben says, frank and open. "Rockers are the ones who get the girls. And Ari's still holding out hope that he'll get"—he shoots me a horrible, knowing look—"Sari."

Reena shifts in her seat and pokes at the foam in her drink with a skinny red stirring straw. "Sari." She says it very quietly, like it's a word she's never heard before. Then she doesn't say anything else at all.

I look down at the table's scratched surface. Someone before us has left behind a coffee ring. It's abstract, like a Rothko, something you'd pay about seven zillion dollars for at one of the tiny galleries tucked off in the way downtown, swank scene.

The room suddenly feels four times too small. I'd give anything to be back outside in the sharp, bitter cold again. I glance at my watch for lack of anything else to do.

Holy crap.

I look up. "Sound check's in half an hour."

fifteen

By now I think we've established that, all told, I'm really not so punk rock.

I'm not Sid Vicious. I'm not Lou Reed, I'm not Kurt Cobain, I'm not Frank Black, I'm not Iggy Pop, I'm not Morrissey, Michael Stipe, or Robert Smith. I'm not Robert Plant. I'm not Mick Jones, Mick Jagger, or Mike D.

I'm not even Miley Cyrus.

What I am is possibly about to throw up, freak out, or break down.

It's not good.

The Back Alley isn't packed, not even half as crowded as it was for the Love and Sprockets show. But try telling that to the coffee-sludge still currently churning in my stomach. Caffeine: bad choice.

"It's a decent turnout," Reena says, poking me in the ribs and sending another wave of nausea through my system. She seems to have shaken the Sari thing—whatever that *thing* was, anyway—off. "I mean, enough people. But not so much that I totally want to barf." She is looking a little green, though.

"Just partially?" I tease, because it momentarily makes me feel better. "A fraction of puke?"

She opens her mouth to respond, but the words I hear instead are startlingly incongruent.

"Are you ready to ROCK AND F^&*ING ROLL?" Jonas leaps in front of me and does a terrifying impression of Steven Tyler. I ... can't even. He's sprayed me with a wash of spit and he's for sure going to put someone's eye out with those wayward devil horns. There's no excuse. None.

"Chill *out,* man," I say, blinking and wiping my cheeks.

The bassist from one of the other bands, Tuna Melt, glares at us. And here I thought it was totally kosher to tear it up backstage before a gig.

It's not as though the tension is palpable or anything. For starters, the Tribe is definitely the youngest band here. I mean, we're all wearing those paper bracelets that blatantly announce that we're underage. So there's really no getting around it.

And frankly, no one is exactly intimidated by us. Certainly not Zombie Love Child, a scary headbanger crew who are possibly planning some voodoo worship before their set. Tuna Melt, a White Stripes/Strokes hybrid ripoff, clearly hates us. Not to mention, it's impossible to tell if the two lead vocalists are married or brother and sister. Gross. And then there's Highlands, comprised mainly of languid, disaffected hipsters who may or may not keel over from malnutrition or drunkenness before they even have the chance to take the stage.

You can see how this assortment of rock wannabes might find Jonas' blatant displays of immaturity distasteful.

"Can't you guys get it together?" Reena asks, annoyed. "We're on first. Don't be idiots." Her skin is looking less green, but more blueish white. I don't think that's an improvement, medically speaking.

Right. On first. Forgot about that.

From the eaves of stage left, I can see Ben out there, setting up with Yossi. He holds on to what will be Reena's mic as Yossi adjusts the height.

It's kind of cool to have a roadie. Of course, the fact that our roadie is eleven is doing nothing for our rock 'n' roll image.

"Check. Check. Check." He mouth-breathes into the microphone, but at least there's no feedback. Yossi gives him a satisfied high five, then leads him back to where the rest of us are huddled.

"Leonard says that Ben can stay here while we perform."

"Leonard's the bouncer," Ben explains proudly. He's so

excited about it that I don't have the heart to tell him that this is information we already have.

"You're our groupie, dude!" Jonas reaches out and ruffles Ben's hair in what I guess is a brotherly way.

"Groupies are girls. I mean, if you're a boy. You know, in theory," Reena says, her eyes glittery and dark. "Ben is a roadie. Technically."

"Well, *technically*, I guess you're right." Jonas says. Technically speaking, he might be having some anger issues.

"So we've got our set list," I say, cutting in. We're playing three songs—one cover and two originals. Believe it or not, the originals were written mostly by Reena and Yossi. It turns out the boy's got some poetry in his soul, and she's pretty skilled with matching lyrics and melody. I for one was floored. It's almost enough to make a person want to renounce his ever-present notebook.

Reena steps forward again, smooths her skirt against her hips, and runs through the order of our songs. "Jonas will be on *bass*," she confirms.

"'Course." He nods his head like there was never any question.

The main room goes quiet, suddenly, and then we hear a low cheer, followed by the announcer giving the lineup for the battle. *Now* the tension is palpable. Maybe only for me, but still. I could definitely partially puke, right about now. I'm focused on the stage, but out of the corner of my eye I see the head Tuna Melt sidle up to Reena. He offers her something, a sip of a bottle. She levels him with a look, declines.

"I'll take it, man," Jonas offers, only to be ignored.

I might be a fan of Tuna Melt.

"You guys are the high school band, right?" Tuna asks in a whisper that's more of a speaking voice.

Reena nods.

"The ones who got added at the last minute?"

Another quick, sharp bob of assent.

"Cool."

Tuna Melt thinks we're cool. I'm totally going to pick up their demo after the battle is over. Big fan, that's me. I'd be a groupie, if I were a girl.

"I guess that would explain why there are so many high school kids out there."

There are?

I'm too freaked out by this news to be offended by Tuna's implications. Whatever fraction of my body was about to combust is now joined by the remainder of my nervous system. I glance quickly at my bandmates to discover that they're definitely experiencing the same thing. Reena looks like she might be reconsidering that shot of whatever Tuna Melt had shoved her way just seconds ago. Yossi is attempting to furiously chew off the top layer of his lip. Even Jonas looks ruffled—there's the tiniest of sheen forming around the tips of his oh-so-careful sideburns.

We're about to collectively lose it. I have to take charge.

I step forward. "You guys—" My voice makes a tragic squeaking sound. Not quite as commanding as I'd hoped.

I clear my throat, try again.

"You guys, this is awesome. It means our fans are out there." Such as they are. "They're here to support us."

"He's right," Reena chimes in, the color slowly returning to her cheeks. "It means we've got a receptive crowd. This should make us less nervous, not more."

Jonas wrinkles his forehead and winks at us carelessly. "Who's nervous?" He runs his hand through his hair, taking extreme care not to muss the perfectly sculpted tufts. "Guys," he says, leaning in and leering. "We're going to totally kick ass."

And for once, I'm in total agreement with Jonas Fein.

• • •

We do. Kick ass, I mean. We get out there, and it's like something comes over us.

Reena's probably right, in that we've got this crazy-receptive crowd and stuff, but to be honest, that's not even really it. The truth is that from where I stand on the stage, I can't even see the crowd, just a mash of faces and mouths and fists, disparate images that swim between the bobbing lights of this dim, rickety room.

It's more of a trance thing, like the moment we step out the blood rushes into my ears and I have a moment of wooziness, and then … stillness. I've got my guitar, and the rest of the band is in place, and we all have our set down, and we all totally *want* this, like it's the first time we've all ever wanted the same exact thing at the same exact time. And all of that tension that we had between us... well, I don't want to say that it melts away or anything, because that's not exactly right, but it's more that... we *feed* on it, I guess. We use it. Like that tension, that anger, that awkwardness, weirdness, or whatever you want to call it, is some kind of battery that we're all plugged into. And it works. *We* work. And like I say—we totally kick ass.

• • •

Apparently we don't kick quite as much ass as Highlands, which, I don't know, might have something to do with the lead singer's extremely mini skirt. Not that I'm bitter. We come in second, which is seriously so much more than I expected.

Of course, second place doesn't get the big dramatic encore, so we're backstage reveling in our silver medal status as Highlands takes the stage again, miniskirt and all.

"F^&*ing-*A*! Second! We rule!" Jonas contorts into a series of fist-pumps.

For a moment I want to remind him that technically, as second place, we really *don't* rule, but I'm feeling so good that I decide not to ruin the post-set glow we've all got going on. Even Yossi looks fairly pleased with himself, bobbing his head up and down in time to what we can hear of Highlands.

"Nice job," Tuna Melt sleazes, wandering over to our

tight little unit of self-congratulation. This time he's got two shot glasses in his hand, one of which he tilts toward Reena.

Not that I'm, like, the boss of Reena or anything, but isn't that illegal? Not the shots (although they are, but whatever)—I mean the fact that this dude must be at least twenty-five. I mean, we're talking *old.*

Reena shakes her head no at the drinks. I feel a wave of inexplicable relief, and then, quick as lightning, Jonas snatches one of the short, skinny glasses out of Tuna's hand and downs it in one gulp.

He is seriously going to get himself pummeled. And I'm just going to watch.

It's a nice fantasy.

Tuna's mouth opens in surprise, but before he can get a word out, we're surrounded by a flurry of giggles, hair spray, and orange tic tacs.

"Baby!" I catch a flash of blonde curls, see a set of extremely pointy, hot pink fingernails fling themselves around Jonas' neck, hear the distinctive smacks of an extremely enthusiastic kiss hello.

Larafromcamp. In the flesh.

I think we all secretly suspected that she was like the Loch Ness Monster, or Bigfoot, or a unicorn or something. That she didn't quite exist. But here she stands, reeking of the perfume samples that slip out of my mother's magazines sometimes, a vision in stretch denim.

Jonas steps back and holds her at arms' length. "You're here!"

She rolls her eyes. "Of *course.* And I brought some friends from school." She waves vaguely toward some generic brunettes hovering awkwardly nearby, brandishing fringed leather bags like talismans.

"Cool." A new voice, and more girlie vapors, this time that vanilla lip-glossy stuff that I know...

That I know that *Sari* wears.

"You guys were *so amazing,*" Sari purrs, moving just slightly closer to Jonas, close enough to spark the most minute pitch of eyebrow arch in Larafromcamp. I think they might be operating on some female frequency, some unspoken language of the double X chromosomes. It's one part intoxicating, one part utterly terrifying.

I push the terror part aside. I mean—Sari's *here.*

"Don't you have the SATs tomorrow?" I blurt, in a moment of shameless, unplanned dorkitude.

She shrugs. "I'm gonna have to retake them at least once anyway, right?"

Girl makes a good point. I like it.

"So," she says. "There are a bunch of us from Gittleman here. And we want to celebrate."

"We're down," Jonas says, earning himself a sidelong but undeniably dirty look from Larafromcamp.

"My parents are out of town," Sari goes on. "So we were thinking we'd all go back to my place. For an after party."

Jonas smirks. Reena shrugs. Yossi blinks.

Lara's eyebrows go up once again, this time in perfect tandem. She places one of those immaculately manicured nails flat against Jonas' chest, marking her territory in a most unsubtle fashion.

"Awesome," she says. "Let's go."

sixteen

There's a whole thing about carpools, and who's going with whom, but in the end it's decided that Yossi, Jonas, and I are going with the equipment (and with Ben, who's a little bit like equipment in that I'm responsible for him, though he's definitely more animated than a guitar case or an amp) in Yossi's car. This leaves Reena to cuddle up to Sari, Lara, and the Lara-ettes, but she assures us it's cool. (I have my doubts, but can't bring myself to get into it then and there. I mean, she's a big girl, right?)

We load up the car, tell the girls we'll see them at Sari's, and pile in, thundering heavily—but desperately slowly—down Houston Street and toward the Holland Tunnel.

It is unfortunate but true, and it must be said: Yossi drives like a senior citizen. A *sedated* senior citizen.

Meanwhile, that energy we were feeling back in the club is definitely still with us. My blood tingles in my veins. Jonas pops some Good Charlotte in the CD player and I don't take it out. In fact, I'm charitable enough that I give a little hum or two under my breath.

"Yeah, man," Jonas says, reaching forward and adjusting the volume. "Crank it up." I assume he's talking to himself. Whatever.

Unexpectedly, though, Yossi steps in, fiddling with the radio buttons until the car goes quiet again. "Come on," he says. "I can't concentrate. My ears are still ringing from the Back Alley."

"F^&* *yeah,* they're ringing!" Jonas shouts, and beats out an explosive rhythm against the dashboard with the palms of his hands. I wince. That has to hurt. It definitely hurts *me.*

The car swerves slightly. "I'm serious," Yossi says quietly, but none of us are listening.

Ben sits straight up in his seat, launching into his fiercest air guitar. Bear claws all over the place. "Sex Pistols!" he says, laughing giddily at the "s" word. You can just tell he's been waiting for hours to drop that one. "Come on, Yossi, can't we listen to the Sex Pistols? You've got to have them."

"What do you know about the Sex Pistols?" Jonas scoffs, twisting in his seat so his upper torso is practically squashed in between Ben and me in the back.

"Kid knows more than you do," I reply truthfully, cheerfully. He's been a good roadie tonight and a decent wingman before that, so I have to give Ben credit where it's due.

"NO!" Yossi shouts suddenly, cutting us all off.

We each stop, stock-still in our places because it goes without saying that Yossi is so not the outburst type. He smacks at the radio again, and now the car goes completely silent except for the sound of his breathing.

"I told you," he says. "I can't concentrate."

After that it gets quiet in the car, as we pass through the tunnel and cross the narrow, dark divide back to our boring, suburban, anonymous high school lives.

• • •

Of course, Jonas can't stay silent for more than six minutes at a time—he's got the attention span of a cocker spaniel, that kid—and also, I don't think any of us (with the possible exception of Yossi) are quite ready to go back to being plain old Gittle-men again just yet.

At least we've still got Sari's party, as far as postponing the inevitable goes.

"We need to stop, man, before we get there," Jonas says. I can practically hear Yossi grit his teeth, even from all the way in the back seat of the car. "We need to pick up beer."

I snort. "With what? Your library card?"

As if Jonas even has a library card.

"Come on," Jonas says. "There's gotta be some cute lonely chick working a 7-Eleven around here."

I laugh. "And she's going to sell you beer? How lonely do you think she is?" I glance at Ben. "Cover your ears," I suggest. He does, reluctantly.

Jonas turns and shoots me a dirty look. "Fine. Whatever. But we at least have to pick up snacks or something. I'm starving."

"I am, too," Ben pipes in, looking immediately abashed. Like it's some sort of capital crime to be hungry.

Which, I realize suddenly, I am as well. No, I'm more than hungry. I'm *ravenous.*

"We do need food," I agree.

"Fine. Food," Yossi says tightly. "But it's almost eleven. I'm not staying at the party for very long."

"Okay, Rabbi Gluck," Jonas snaps. Which kind of doesn't even make sense, but whatever. Jonas takes his own cue, turns the CD back on, and the car is bathed in sunny pop music yet again.

Annoyance radiates from the driver's seat, but Yossi is silent. Good Charlotte gives way to the Get Up Kids, which may be emo but is at least more respectable than some Top Forty crap.

Ben air guitars. Jonas drums. I hum my heart out.

Yossi sees a convenience store up ahead on the right and does a whole big show of turning on his blinker and adjusting his mirror and checking his blind spot and whatever else an extremely cautious, responsible person does as he merges ever-so-carefully into the right lane. If the speed limit is twenty-five, he's doing nineteen. *Maybe* twenty. He could be a driver's ed instructor. It's that sad.

Jonas' cell phone shrieks out an electronic rendition of Offspring's "Self Esteem" and I twitch and almost vomit. Ben finds this to be hilarious. Jonas dives into his messenger bag, tossing items out frenetically in a desperate search for the phone: a long-sleeved tee shirt, an iPod shuffle, an SAT vocab booklet—shocking—a can of Red Bull—until, triumphantly, he finds what he's looking for, answers the phone, and mercifully puts a stop to the very questionable cover of some questionable-enough-to-begin-with music.

"Babe!" he shouts, doing his best *Swingers.* "You're there?" He turns to us. "It's Lara. They're *there* already. At the party." Back into the receiver he does his party-voice again: "*Awesome*! Yeah, we'll be there soon. Just picking up some—holy f^&*, that is a sick car—guys!—look at that car! I think it's a—"

He gestures wildly with his free hand. We all turn our heads, dutifully entranced.

It's an Aston Martin, is what it is, parked smack dab in the convenience store parking lot, and it *is* pretty sick. Even Yossi has the good grace to be impressed. I'd kind of like to meet the sucker who takes a car like this on a late-night ice cream run.

"I gotta go," Jonas yells at the phone. "We're here. And I want to take a picture of this car."

Between Jonas, the music, Ben laughing, and, to be

honest, me gawping, things have gotten a little chaotic. Still, though, Yossi manages to tune us all out. He's turning the heck out of his wheel, cutting one way, backing up, cutting the wheel again, a look of fierce concentration on his face. There's so much going on that at first, when it happens, I don't even hear it. But then it's back, and louder:

The unmistakable crunch of metal against metal, of Yossi's bumper groaning against another car's door.

Against *the* car door. The Aston Martin.

Yossi gasps, puts the car in park, and scrambles out to survey the damage. Ben follows, mouth agape.

I put my hand on Jonas' arm as he reaches for his door handle.

"Don't," I say. "Don't take a picture of this."

• • •

"Oh God," Jonas says, stalking in a circle around the periphery of the scary-fancy car. Miraculously, no alarm's gone off, but that's about it as far as divine intervention extends here. There's a big ugly scar running down the back left door of this car. Whereas Yossi's bumper has only picked up a fleck or two of chipped paint. "Oh, f^&*. Oh, God, God, God."

"Enough," Yossi says. He's surprisingly calm, all things considered. "God's got nothing to do with this."

That's true enough. And on the off chance that He is up there somehow watching all this? Well then, there's no sense in getting Him all riled up. Too little, too late and whatever.

"Okay, well, forget the food, man," Jonas says, starting to sounding panicky. "We've gotta get out of here."

Yossi shakes his head. "We can't hit and run."

We can't. I mean, of course, we *can't.*

Right?

Jonas shrugs. "It's *not* a hit and run. Not really. This is a parked car. It doesn't even count as an accident. It's barely a scratch. Totally barely a scratch."

"Oh, uh, come on," I have to say. Because—uh, *come on.*

"So what are we going to do? Wait here until the driver comes out, and get our asses kicked?" It's a persuasive argument. Jonas makes a damn good point.

"At least I have to exchange insurance information," Yossi protests.

"What's to exchange? You hit a *parked car.* This is going to be on you, bro. And it's gonna cost some cizz-nash," Jonas says.

It figures that the one time he'd be right about something, it'd be this. Even if he does sound ridiculous—he's right.

"Biggie's right," I echo, sounding ridiculous myself. Ridiculous and gross.

"What?" Yossi turns to face me. "You think we should just leave?" His expression is one of challenge, disbelief. How could I have ever thought that Yossi's big, round face was expressionless? I've never seen so many expressions cross one person's face at a time.

"No, it's just ... "

It's just that we're gonna be in serious trouble.

"It's just that we're gonna be in *serious* f^&*ing trouble."

Jonas and I are in sync? If I thought it was eerie when Reena said exactly what I was thinking, then this is downright bone-chilling.

"But still ... " I say to Jonas, not sure whose side I'm arguing anymore.

"You can't leave the scene of an accident," Ben says, sounding extremely Public Service Announcement-y. It doesn't help that somewhere inside me—not even that deep inside, really—I know he's right.

"You can if it's not really an accident," Jonas insists. "But we're running out of time. Whoever the driver of this car is, he's going to be out of the store and back here with us any second." He indicates toward a man in a well-tailored coat whose silhouette we can see through the storefront. A likely candidate for the owner of the car. Forking over his cash and sure to be on his way outside in seconds.

"Jonas ... " I'm really not offering anything helpful to the mix right now. Repeating everyone's names or the last few words they said is not exactly useful. But it's just about all that I can manage.

Jonas levels me with his most solemn gaze. "Ari, dude—your parents don't know what you're doing tonight, right?"

My stomach sinks because of course, they don't. I know

where Jonas is going with this. And I kind of hate myself for doing so … but I have to sort of agree with him.

"No," I admit grudgingly.

"And they would be pissed if they found out?"

To say the least. "Um, yeah."

Jonas jerks his head insistently toward Yossi's car. "Then dude, we've got to get out of here. Like, *now.*"

I glance from Jonas to Yossi and back to Jonas. Ben watches me watch them. I feel sick.

The dude in the coat fumbles with his wallet, stashes his change. He's almost out the door, almost about to discover what we've done to his car.

But, like clockwork, the three of us dive back into the car.

I kind of can't believe us.

As we buckle ourselves in (safety first!), Yossi swoops into the drivers' side and digs up a handful of … stuff from the console. Oh—it's a pen and a scrap of paper. He scribbles something on the paper, then rushes to slide it under the windshield of the Aston Martin.

Still no alarms. Maybe Yossi's onto something with the whole God-thing, after all. It certainly seems like he's got an in with someone up there.

He jumps back into the car as hastily as he can manage, and peels out—carefully, especially now.

He looks just as disgusted with himself as I feel.

"What was that?" I ask. "You know—the paper."

He doesn't take his eyes off of the road. He clutches the

steering wheel with shiny white knuckles. "I left a note," he says. "With my information."

I nod. Of course he left a note.

"Of *course* you f^&*ing left a note!" Jonas cackles, slapping against the dashboard in hysterics. "You are *such* a *mensch*! Such a f^&*ing *rabbi*!"

He's laughing so hard he starts to hiccup. Ben glances at me, clearly not sure how to take this reaction.

I want to be stoic, unresponsive, disapproving. I want to set an example for Ben, to create as much distance as possible between myself and Jonas and the terrible knot settling somewhere deep in my stomach.

But I can't.

I truly can't. I don't know if it's fallout hysteria from the stress of possibly being beaten to death by an extremely wealthy licensed driver, or if I've just spent too much of the day too freaked out about my not-date and rethinking my life goals as a cooler-than-thou musician, or if I'm still on some weird post-performance head trip, or if I'm secretly convinced that playing a gig the night before the SATS is the most self-destructive thing I've ever done—or if it's somehow all of those things. Because those are kind of a lot of things, and they're all a tangle, somewhere at the back of my throat.

My throat, my stomach... and now my head's spinning. I am a medical mystery, a walking disaster. Except, I'm *not even walking*. I am sitting. In the back seat of Yossi Gluck's car. And I am falling apart.

Man, that's lame.

The whole thing is so lame that, yeah, I can't stop myself. It builds in me like a wave, a geyser, or some other watery thing that means huge, streaming pressure. If I weren't buckled into my leather-upholstered seat, I'd shoot straight up and through the moon roof.

I laugh.

No, that's not even accurate. "Laughing" is too tame, too innocuous a descriptor for what I'm doing. I'm chortling, I'm guffawing, I'm snorting and swallowing. Tears stream down my face. I bang on the back of Jonas' seat, which makes him slap the dashboard even harder. Our laughter mixes, becomes a force unto itself, something that wraps itself around our necks and squeezes until we can't see straight.

I'm dizzy. I can't see straight. And yeah—I'm still pretty sickened by myself.

But I can't stop.

seventeen

I've always secretly thought that Sari Horowitz must live in a big, fluffy pink castle or something, that there should be a moat, or a trapdoor made of solid gold leading to the entrance to her house. Rose petals dripping out the window of her bedroom, fireworks set to release every twenty-two minutes or whatever. It just goes to show how much I worship her—it's much deeper than your typical cheesy high school crush; it's become something appallingly literal.

And yet.

When we pull up to her house (Jonas knows exactly

where it is, of course, and I can't bring myself to ask him how many times he's been here before), I am somewhat disappointed to find it blandly average. It's a modest split-level, painted either off-white or a white-white that has seen better days. There are no rose petals, though an enormous potted plant rests just in front of the screen door, wilting balefully. The entire vibe is one of misplaced optimism and middle-class distraction.

Generally speaking, I can relate.

And while we're on the subject of misplaced optimism—after my bout of spontaneous hysteria, things got quiet again in the car. We haven't really recovered since then, not that you'd know it from the way Jonas is behaving. He really does have no shame. Either he's that oblivious or just that full of himself—and I'm seriously not sure which.

I pause on Sari's doorstep, partly from nervousness, but partly wanting to savor the moment. I'm here. I'm actually here, at her house, at her invitation.

Never mind that she actually invited the whole junior class over. I'm not going to let that kill my buzz.

"Dude, what're you waiting for?" Jonas shoves past me and pushes the door open, not even bothering to try the bell. "There're *hot girls* inside."

Another excellent point.

I venture cautiously in behind him, with Ben ("cover your ears, and maybe your eyes") and Yossi at my heels (demonstrating dramatically varying levels of enthusiasm).

Whatever lackluster normalcy Sari's house radiated externally, inside it's a completely different story.

I feel as though I've stepped into a movie, something funky and retro and deliciously ironic where guys in band tee shirts sip from huge plastic cups and make passes at girls wearing multiple tank tops. The noise level is high, but unified; all of the chatter together creates a pleasant hum that brings me back to the hours before our crime spree, back when we were—when *I* was—the Tribe, a member of the Tribe, *the* member of the Tribe. When we were cool.

Here now, at Sari's, we're cool again. I mean, first off, as I have mentioned—we're at *Sari's.* But more than that—so is *everyone else.* Like tons of kids from school. And they're here for *us.*

Case in point: a cold can slick with moisture is pressed into my hand. I look up. It's Melissa Mendel.

"*Great* set, Ari," she says. "I totally thought you guys should have won."

I glance down at the drink in my hand. Bud Light. I'm sure I've made my thoughts on the matter of Bud Light pretty clear, but what the hey, it's a party. I pop the top open and swig. "Yeah?" I gulp. I'm thirsty, after all. "I thought so, too."

She shrieks with the laughter of the truly possessed. I smile warily and take one step back. Then I think better of it. She's a fan, and I can't deny my adoring public, after all.

"Some party," I say, choking down some more beer.

It's nasty, like acidic water or something worse, but it's beer and I'm a rock star now. I have an image to uphold.

"Right?" Melissa draws out the one syllable until it's more like three. "Everyone came." She steps back and waves as if demonstrating just exactly who "everyone" is.

It is kind of a lot of people.

I catch Reena turning a corner, heading into what looks like the kitchen from where I stand. She looks up, making eye contact, then sticks her tongue out at me, and I grin back.

Melissa steps forward and grabs at my forearm, almost possessive, territorial. "I had *no idea* Reena had such a good voice," she coos, smiling so widely that I can see her molars.

"Well, she used to be in the Hanukkah choir."

More maniacal laughter. I'm stunned. Melissa Mendel may not be my dream girl—hell, she's not even my daydream girl or even my occasional stray thought girl—but she's cute, and she's popular, and—no doubt about it—she is into me. Or if she's not into me *qua* me, then she is digging on the Tribe. And I can't help but take it personally, you know? Right now, I can't think of a better plan for the evening.

Yossi strides past me with Ben at his side, and I feel a nagging flash of... *something*. I turn, but before I can call out, say something, Melissa is flanked by an army of alphas—some girls, glittery and giggly and swathed in extremely stretchy denim, and some guys, who are taller, tougher, and full of swagger. All of whom seem, inexplicably, interested in *me.*

"Tell us about the show."

"We heard you *rocked,* man!"

"Ari, you were so cute with the guitar. How long have you been playing the guitar?"

I don't know if it's a confidence born of having spent the day trawling the city with a bad-ass indie chick, or rocking out at the Back Alley, or maybe even the lite beer, but I am totally in my element. Everyone wants to hear what I've got to say—and I've got a *lot* to say.

The story about Yossi's accident, for example? That kills.

"He insisted—*insisted*—on leaving a note!"

"Dude, man—Jonas really called him a rabbi?" Snickers, chortles, muffled, drunken walla.

"*Dude,* I mean, it's right, you know? It's, like, perfect."

"True!" Melissa claps a delicate hand over glossy lips. "So true. Perfect."

It's perfect. *I'm* perfect. This is the perfect night.

In fact, I'm feeling so great, so on top of my game, that after a few more lite beers and some ego-stroking from Melissa et al., I decide to make my move. It's time. Time to tell Sari how I *really* feel about her.

She'll be cool about it. I'm sure of it. Hell, she'll be *psyched.* I'm in a band. A good band. A band whose music is on tonight's party shuffle, that Sari herself (presumably) loaded.

I grab myself another drink (the lite beer is starting to grow on me) and weave my way through the masses of bodies tangled in thick pockets across the sprawling house. Reena, Yossi, and—get this—Ben are seated at the Horowitz kitchen table, playing something that looks suspiciously like Gin Rummy. Can you even play Gin Rummy with three people? And should you, at a house party?

Ben looks at me and pantomimes cupping his hands over his ears. I smile. It's his way of telling me he's doing his part, he's staying out of trouble. And anyway, I don't have time to worry about that. Not now. Sari is somewhere in this house. I'm like a heat-seeking missile on a mission.

I stomp from room to room with purpose. She's not in the living room—no one is, actually; it's been sealed off through a complicated system of folding chairs, which makes a point. She's not in the basement (although some other people are, and in various stages of undress, which is sort of awkward for all of us); she's not in the kitchen or the dining room, where I've just been.

Is she upstairs? The upstairs looks to be cordoned off, although the elaborate folding-chair thing has been disrupted in such a way to suggest that at least one person has violated the party boundaries. A flash of hot pink manicure radiates in my periphery and I whirl.

"Larafr—*Lara,* have you seen Sari?"

She shakes her head emphatically, drunkenly. "Haven't. 'Ve you seen Jonas?"

"Uh-uh." Do I sound as wasted as she does? Probably. Oh well.

"I was gonna go upstairs. But s'looks like we can't." She motions to the chairs, respectful, even in her inebriation, of the party boundaries I mentioned.

"Right. I'm gonna go anyway." I give her the thumbs up. Like I'm Indiana Jones or Anakin Skywalker or some other action hero-y guy. "I'll let you know."

She tries to wink but briefly forgets to open her eye again. I don't really have time to deal with it.

Up the stairs—there are a *lot* of stairs, and they're polished and wooden, a death trap for hardcore partiers. Down the hall and into one—okay, no, that's a bathroom, and it's in use, whoops ... To the right—is a linen closet, shockingly, Sari is not to be found there. I crack one bedroom door squeamishly (I've already had more than an eyeful of some of my classmates tonight, unfortunately for all parties involved). Empty. The next bedroom, also empty.

There's only one more door on this floor, and I suspect it leads to the master bedroom. I can't think of any reason why Sari would be in the master bedroom, but unless she's hiding in the fireplace or in the washing machine, there's nowhere else left to look.

I swallow the rest of my beer in one long pull. Liquid courage. I breathe, count to three in my head.

I push the door to the bedroom open.

I drop my can of beer.

The can's empty, so it doesn't make too much of a clatter—just a tinny clanging sound as it skitters down the hallway behind me.

From where she lies on her parents' bed, Sari doesn't even flinch.

It's possible she didn't hear the can drop. What with how Jonas is lying on top of her, his tongue shoved into her ear.

"MOTHERF^&*ER!"

Okay. *That,* she heard. That, I think her next door neighbors heard.

"Jesus, Ari, what the f^&*?" Jonas leaps off her and runs his hands through his hair. Always the hair with Jonas.

"Um, Ari." Sari does not look pleased at this interruption. "What's up?"

"What's up? What's *up*?" I'm seeing spots, stars, torrents, waves of anger washing in front of my eyes. The liquid courage has metabolized into a slow, viscous rage. "What do you mean, what's up? I was looking for you." The accusation in my voice is unattractive, I can tell. Even to my own ears.

"Here I am," she says uncertainly. "But, um ..."

"Dude, man, can you maybe give us some privacy?" Jonas shoots me a crooked grin, like he's sure there's nothing in the world that I'd rather do.

"You asshole. Your *girlfriend* is looking for you."

Sari has the good grace to look slightly ashamed. Jonas mostly just looks confused. But when I turn to get the hell out of the room, at least they both follow.

• • •

Somewhere, on some subconscious level, I'm pretty aware that I'm throwing a full-on post-pubescent temper tantrum. But much like with my breakdown in the car, I can't seem to help myself. Chalk it up to pressure, disappointment, or even something as basic and dumb as drunkenness, but I am furious in an all-encompassing, throw-something-out-the-window-and-possibly-bust-some-skulls kind of way. It's a very unusual sensation for someone as passive as me.

I storm into the kitchen and grab Ben by the elbow.

"We're leaving."

"But I'm winning—ow!" He shakes me off and slaps a card down on the table. "I covered my ears, Ari!"

"*Now*," I say, my voice low.

"Yossi drove us," Ben points out.

"Yossi will drive us home. I'm sure he's ready to leave." Since I'm pretty sure that he was never interested in coming to begin with.

"What's your deal?" Reena asks, puzzled.

"Ask Jonas."

"You found Jonas?" Lara pipes up. She's hunched against the refrigerator, puzzling out some magnetic poetry and slurping at a bright green wine cooler. Her eyeliner has smeared in runny streaks that have settled into the hollows under her eyes. She is considerably less hot under these circumstances than photographic evidence would suggest.

There's a tiny voice chilling out in the back of my brain, sort of propped up on the occipital lobe back there, and it's telling me to shut it. To just leave things alone. But I can't. I just can't.

"I found Jonas. And Sari," I say, my voice heavy with meaning.

Lara shrieks and drops her wine cooler. The bottle shatters.

"Perfect," Reena says, rolling her eyes and jumping out of her seat. "No—don't worry, Ari. I've got it." She roots around under the kitchen sink for some paper towels and starts wiping things up.

A shadow appears in the kitchen doorway, followed by another.

"Jonas," Lara slurs. She runs up to him and pushes him squarely in the middle of his chest. "You were upstairs with *her*?"

"Yeah," Sari says. Her face is a mixture of satisfaction and fear, which seems ... just about right, actually. Honestly.

"I came ... on the *bus* ... to see your show!" Lara sputters, her face red and sweaty. "I brought *friends*!"

I have to give it to her—a bus trip to the city is definitely a testament of devotion.

So what does that say about my train ride with Reena?

No—this isn't about Reena. This is about Sari. And *Jonas.*

Focus.

Jonas shrugs, like he's just so damn in demand and all that, and what can you even do about it.

"Babe, I know, and I'm so glad to see you. But the

thing about me and Sari is ... well, there's been something building for a while."

There *has*?

"What are you talking about, man? How can anything build when you have a girlfriend? I thought you were so into Lara. She's all you ever talk about!"

Lara looks like she's going to cry, or barf, or possibly both, and it occurs to me that her feelings are real, actual. That she's the one who has been genuinely betrayed by Jonas.

Unlike me and my imaginary connection to Sari.

That doesn't take the sting away, though. It doesn't make my anger any less acute. Any less *now.*

"It has. Been ... you know ... I don't know. Building. There's something there." Sari speaks slowly, like it's dawning on her, too, how crushed and cruddy Lara must feel.

The Lara-ettes edge their way into the kitchen, glaring at Sari and pouting in Lara's direction like extremely sympathetic backup dancers.

"What about ... " I trail off. What about what? What do Sari and I have, anyway? "What about the tutoring?"

She stares at me, her eyes round and full. "Ari, I'm failing Calculus."

Yeah.

The funny thing is, I knew that.

And that little voice, that asshat hanging out in the back of my brain? *He* knew that, too. All this time. But he was hoping otherwise. He was desperately hoping for a different outcome.

Fat f^&*ing chance. That's not how things work for the Aris of this world. The Jonases, sure. But not the Aris.

F^&* it.

I hurl myself at Jonas and grab him by the edges of his frayed f^&*ing fake–vintage, mock-indie, post-grunge flannel shirt. "I'm going to f^&*ing kill you," I say, meaning it.

He shoves me. Not lightly.

I wind up. The last time I physically fought with anyone, it was Markowitz, and it was during third-grade recess. Something involving GI Joes, I think. But I guess it's all just innate. I'm going to knock every single one of Jonas' stupid f^&*ing teeth right down his throat.

I release, but—

My arm stops, My fist freezes, mid-trajectory. Someone's got me. *Yossi's* got me.

"Let me go, man."

I shrug and wiggle, and suddenly I'm free. But before I can launch myself at Jonas again, Yossi's face pops up between us.

"What," he says, his voice trembling with emotion, "are you guys doing?"

"Stay out of it," I say.

"Leave it alone, rabbi," Jonas spits.

"You know what?" Yossi asks, stretching his arms out

on either side of him so that Jonas and I are both forced to take a step back. "No."

Jonas snorts. "No? What're you gonna do? Pray for me?"

"No," Yossi says. "I wouldn't bother with that. You're not worth it."

Okay, wow. Huh.

Jonas folds his arms over his chest. "What the f^&* does that even mean?"

"Just what I said, Jonas. You're not worth it. What would be the point in praying for you? You don't believe in prayer."

"I don't believe in lame-ass religious school bull—"

"Forget religious school rhetoric. That's not what this is about. No one's asking you to read Rambam in your spare time. Half the kids in Gittleman couldn't care less about Judaism. You think I don't know that? You think I don't know that even by yeshiva standards, I'm considered some kind of Torah-thumping freakshow?"

I swallow. That's putting it kind of harshly. But still.

Yossi breathes deeply. "But if you had even the slightest ounce of spirituality in you, you'd know that prayer is about two things: self-reflection and connection."

"Connect this." Jonas makes an extremely lewd gesture.

"That's just it. It's got nothing to do with prayer, or Judaism, or rabbinics. It's just about being a human being. And you don't even get it."

"Who are you to judge?" Jonas looks seriously pissed,

which is surprising. I never would have guessed that Yossi would be able to get under Jonas' skin.

"He's right, man," I say, feeling smug. My drunken haze is clearing, and now all I feel is sweaty and deflated. "I mean, he *does* read Rambam in his spare time. So he would know."

"Give it up, Ari," Yossi says with disgust. "Jonas worships himself, fine, it's true. But you? You don't worship anything. Jonas may be egotistical, but you have no idea who you are at all. It's really pathetic."

I open my mouth, then close it.

"F^&* you, Yossi," I say finally.

"You can get another ride home," he says, perfectly calm and together.

He turns to his sister, who's been uncharacteristically silent through this whole titanic clash. "You ready to go?"

Her shoulders bunch up by her ears. "Uh, actually..." She shoots a glance in the direction of the den, where a few heads pop around the doorway, clearly listening in but pretending in vain to be absorbed in their own conversations. "I think Kevin's going to drive me home in a little bit."

Kevin? Kevin Bluestein? The *sophomore*?

Since when does Reena hang out with Kevin Bluestein?

And why the *f^&** do I care?

Bile rises in my throat, sharp and black. I shake my head at Jonas, at Yossi, at Reena.

"Perfect," I say. "Perfect."
And then I say something else:
"Fuck you all."

eighteen

Have you ever taken a standardized test on four hours of sleep and a raging Bud Light hangover? I don't recommend it.

ARI is to SATS as SARI is to CALCULUS.

ARI is to DEAD as JONAS is to ASSHAT.

ARI is to TIRED as REENA is to GONE.

ARI is to OVER IT as YOSSI is to FED UP.

ARI is NAPPING.

• • •

My nap lasts until around 4:00 PM. It's more of a coma, really, though thankfully the parents think I'm recovering from the ninth circle of hell that is multiple choice testing. They'd cry—or worse—if they knew I still had watered-down beer oozing from my pores in slow release.

My cell phone rings at 4:13, waking me. It's not pretty. My tongue is glued to the roof of my mouth and my eyelids feel like they've been Scotch-taped shut from the inside. The phone, which has been digging sharply into me from my back pocket, vibrates and I grab for it.

Jonas.

We barely exchanged three words on our way to the test today, and avoided each others' gazes like we were getting paid for it. What can I say—last night was, um, weird. I couldn't go back to my house or my parents would have figured out that something was up. Staying at Chez Gluck was clearly out of the question. Once the debris had cleared from our massive smackdown, Jonas sheepishly offered for Ben and me to stay at his place, as per the original plan.

Lara slept on the couch, her friends fanned out on the living room floor like wheel spokes covered in lumps of bedding. I guessed they planned to take the train back home at some point today. I didn't ask. Last I saw Lara, she was snoring indelicately, one pasty arm flung across her face. I have a feeling I won't be seeing her again for some time, if ever.

But yeah, the phone. Still ringing. Still Jonas. I pick it up, not without hesitation.

"Yeah?"

"How do you think you did, man?"

"You kidding? I tanked it. The parents are going to lose it."

Jonas laughs shortly. "Well, if your scores suck, at least you know you won't get into Brandeis."

Silver lining. And yet, "That's really not an option." To say the least. I decide to change the subject. "Did Lara go home?"

"The 2:10 from Highland Avenue," he confirms. He pauses. "She was pretty pissed."

"Uh, yeah."

"I think we broke up."

"Huh." Is there something else I should say to this? Some other reaction I should be having?

"But, you know, it's okay, man . . . " He takes a breath, like he's thinking things over. "Long distance relationships suck, you know?"

I don't, really. But, "Yeah."

There's a long silence, during which at least thirty-seven questions race through my brain, but I can't bring myself to choke any of them out. It's not even that I don't want to know the answers. More like . . . I don't want to hear myself sounding so uncertain. Can't be in that position again, anymore.

Jonas clears his throat. "So, I, uh, just wanted . . . to apologize."

I sit up so quickly I nearly bang my head on the bookshelf above my bed. Jonas apologizing? This is unprecedented behavior. If he were here, I'd make him take a picture of it. "Yeah?"

"Yeah, man. I had no idea how you felt about Sari."

Well, that's just crap. But calling him out seems pointless. We've achieved some sort of delicate balance, despite all of the drama last night. Even when we hate each other, we get each other.

He knew. He totally knew. Which is dicky. But, he's also Jonas. He's always going to be Jonas. Apologizing is kind of the most I can expect from him.

He's Jonas, and I'm me. Which has its own ... implications.

"It's cool," I say.

Because it is. Mostly.

• • •

Jonas tells me that he tried to call Yossi, but Yossi wouldn't pick up his cell or come to the home phone. My efforts to get in touch are met with similar results, unsurprisingly. I'm sitting at my desk, contemplating the relative lameness of sending him an email, when an IM pops up on my computer screen.

WIND_UP_GIRL: U THERE?

ILIKELOUREED: DEFINE "THERE." AWAKE. BARELY. U?

WIND_UP_GIRL: YEAH, SAME. LONG NIGHT. KINDA F^&*ED UP.

What does she mean, "Long night"?

Long night as in, "Long night with Kevin Bluestein"?

Long night as in, "No self-respecting platonic male friend of mine would ever come to blows with their best friend/worst enemy over someone like Sari Horowitz"?

Long night as in, "My brother was totally right about you"?

ILikeLouReed: uh huh.

ILikeLouReed: how's yossi?

Wind_Up_Girl: filled with righteous indignation. I think he's busy dealing with the Aston Martin guy—and my parents. Says he's going to pay for the damage with his bar mitzvah money. So once my mom stops with the faux-hyperventilation, we should be fine.

ILikeLouReed: good good.

Wind_Up_Girl: wanted to know about the test.

ILikeLouReed: my mom's gonna hyperventilate for real.

Wind_Up_Girl: that bad?

ILikeLouReed: probably worse . . .

Wind_Up_Girl: whatever happened with Larafromcamp and jonas?

ILikeLouReed: splitsville.

Wind_Up_Girl: huh. So maybe he and sari . . .

ILikeLouReed: yeah. I guess it makes sense.

I take a moment, consider my next message.

What about you? I type.

What about you and Kevin? Do you guys make sense?
I don't hit send.

WIND_UP_GIRL: GOTTA GO. LOTS OF SHRIEKING AND PHONE RINGING GOING ON DOWNSTAIRS. MUST DUCK AND COVER.

What about you and Kevin?
What about us?

WIND_UP_GIRL: TTYL

I still haven't hit send.

nineteen

I wish I could shake the weekend off more easily, but that's apparently just not my MO. Instead, I spend the week in a state of semi-suspended animation. I mean, I go to school, eat dinner with the parents and Ben when they're around, do my homework, sleep. I take my finals, and I think I do okay on them. Small miracles and whatnot. But there are things I don't really do: talk to Yossi, practice guitar, open my notebook even once.

In my dreams, I'm chased by screaming, multiple-choice bubbles.

The Tribe is legendary at school, of course. Everyone who was at the Battle has told everyone who wasn't all about it, in such a way that those who missed it feel like they missed some huge, musical cusp-y thing, like the Beatles on the Ed Sullivan show, or Woodstock, or the airing of the very first music video on MTV.

Still, even with all of the high fives in the hallways and the comments on our MySpace page, we bandmates mainly stay out of each others' way that first week back. It's like some kind of unspoken agreement that we've got going on between us.

But, I mean, Gittleman is a small school. So it's not like we can totally avoid each other. On Wednesday, as Sari and I are walking out of Elkin's class (she got a B on the final thanks to our tutoring, rock), Jonas leaps up behind her and does the whole "guess who" thing, covering her eyes and all. It's all very giggly and googley and gross and before I know it they're devouring each other's faces whole right there in the hallway.

Adorable, right?

Did I mention that Reena bought me a comic book, back when we spent the afternoon in the Village? She did—she bought me a comic book. Or, excuse me, a *graphic novel* (which is supposed to mean it's fancier/more serious, but to me seems to mainly mean that it's longer/more expensive). Anyway, it's called *The Watchmen*. So I've been reading that at night, when I would otherwise be playing guitar or drawing—er, writing songs.

I'm curled up with *The Watchmen* Wednesday night,

trying to decide what my superhero power would be (I already know Jonas'—the power of persuasion, which he would engage via invisible lasers shooting out from his sideburns), when there's a knock at my door.

The parents.

My mother looms disproportionately large in the doorway. Her power would be some kind of optical illusion, obviously. Or an ability to bend the perception of others.

"Is there something you want to tell us?" She arches an eyebrow.

It's a trick question.

"Um."

"Ari." Dad's turn to chime in.

I'm about to break down, to fall at their feet and confess as to how I've failed the SATs and will spend the remainder of my days alternately scrubbing toilets, flipping burgers, and self-flagellating. Literally, like with thorns and chains and stuff. But then I see Ben's head pop up in between their two bodies in the doorway.

I'm sorry, he mouths.

This can't be good.

My mother strides into my room, coaxing me backwards in an extremely uncomfortable tango. I collapse onto my bed and she slaps something down in my lap.

Oh.

Keeping It Kosher

They may be ¼ *shomer shabbos,* but that doesn't keep these guys from rocking a totally *pareve* party once the sun goes down!

So, apparently Craig Mandelbaum of the *Jewish News* caught the battle of the bands Saturday night. And he's a fan of the Tribe.

Awesome.

The room is extremely quiet. Like, it's the loudest quiet I have ever experienced in my entire life. I wish those screaming multiple-choice bubbles would appear out of thin air. Those guys are soothing.

"Ari—" my father starts, but my mother jumps in before he's even warmed up.

"*What* is this about?"

It's not like I've never envisioned this moment. Believe it or not, I'm prepared. I even have a handful of stock responses at the ready: *Jonas dragged me into it* (even the parents aren't impervious to his laser-beam sideburns); *it's an extra-curricular for my Brandeis transcript; I'm getting independent study credit for it at school*… and I'm ready—*way* more than ready, if we're going to be honest here—to trot one of those out.

But.

Yossi told me that I'm just as bad as Jonas. Jonas has too much self, but I've got… nothing. That I don't know who I am.

It's not true.

I know who I am. I just haven't bothered to share it with anyone, yet.

I may as well start now. With the parents.

I take a deep breath.

"I started a band."

My mother's face crumples, like I've just announced that I brown-bag shellfish for my school lunch every day, or I skin kittens in my spare time.

"A band?" Dad's confused.

"Yeah."

"But—you don't even play an instrument," my mom sputters. "You *quit* piano."

To the parents, quitting piano is kind of like eating shellfish. Or skinning kittens.

"Actually ... " How to break this news? Like a band-aid—one swift motion. "I play guitar. I mean, not that well," I amend. "But I learned. At camp."

Does the fact that I learned guitar at grade-A certified Jewish camp make the whole sordid situation more palatable? More *kosher*? I can't tell.

"Have you been sneaking around?" Dad asks.

I nod. "Some. I mean, last Saturday, yeah."

My mom's eyelids fly up into her hairline. "The night before the SATs?"

"Mom! I can take them again. I'm just a junior."

"Some colleges take the average of both of your scores, rather than just your highest score," she says. "I don't know if that's the case with Brandeis. I didn't expect that this was going to be an issue—"

"Mom."

This is my moment of truth. Sort of a crystallizing situation, if all of those mystics are to be believed.

Of course, the mystics never had to deal with college applications.

Oh dear God. So I haven't prayed for anything since I begged for Jonas to go along with the Tribe. And he did. So maybe I've used up all of my wishes for the year. But I'm gonna go for it anyway. Seeing as how it's a go-for-broke kind of night and all.

"Mom. Dad." I swallow. "I'm not sure that I want to go to Brandeis."

There's that silence again. The one that rushes through your eardrums and crashes against the inside of your skull. I don't mind it now, though. It gives me a minute to collect myself.

I think about a bunch of things: Showing my parents *The Watchmen,* or my notebook, or my guitar. The MySpace page. The back issues of the *Gittleman Star,* where the Tribe has been immortalized (on microfiche, at least).

But you know what? I don't think that's even necessary, now.

Yossi said that I define myself in negative terms—that all I know is what I *don't* want: to be uncool, to be girlfriendless. To be unexpressed. To be ignored.

But that's not the same thing as knowing what you *do* want. Or going for what you want. And telling people what it is that makes you you.

I don't *know* that I'm going to go to NYU, or that I'm ever even going to pick up a guitar again. I don't *know* if reading graphic novels means that someday my own scribbles will actually add up to something larger. I just don't know.

But I finally have an idea.

Which means, I can tell my parents about it. About them. About my ideas. Plural.

So I do, finally. And they listen.

twenty

It's not as though all of a sudden everything changes: the heavens open, the parents and I reach some sort mind-meeting, peace-making thing where we rush off and read the NYU course catalog aloud together every night before we go to bed. That would be too easy, like something out of a movie, or a tidy little narrative music video (early Madonna, maybe? Back when storytelling was more—pardon the pun—in vogue?).

Instead, real life happens in dribs and drabs. It gets portioned out in metered bites, some of which take more digesting than others. It happens frame by frame. Sometimes you get to linger, to soak in the surroundings. Some panels are more about ambiance than action, while others are pure cliffhanger.

Real life is more like a graphic novel that way.

So the whole college thing is kind of a "to be continued" sort of deal for now, where at least the seed has been planted, and now maybe the idea just needs some time to take root in the parents' big, collective consciousness. We're in the sketch stage, the three of us.

But we're all in it together, which is kind of new for us. So I can live with that.

What I can't deal with, unfortunately, are the white spaces, the stuff that happens in between the boxes and outside of the speech bubbles. The things that go unspoken. I've been thinking a lot about what Yossi said at the party, how I'm effectively the absence of action. If I were a drawing, I'd be rendered in negative space.

It's not cool. Not *enough.* Not anymore.

So I decide to pick up my pencil, so to speak, and return to the drawing board. Or the sheet music, really.

I ask the band to meet me.

• • •

Yossi is worried about time. I can tell.

I mean, it's not like I'm some crazed super-sleuth or anything—he's been glancing at his watch with the panicked expression of a drowning man just about every four seconds since we first arrived here, back at the Forum.

I'm trying not to take it personally. The sun goes down in T-minus one hundred and twenty-two minutes. Shabbos. And I get it—Yossi has somewhere he needs to be. Finally, I really do get it.

I keep it brief. "The article in the *Jewish News* rocked."

"F^&*ing-A," Jonas says, but he's lost some of his usual fire. Like me, he seems unnaturally aware of Yossi's entire state of being. And concerned about it.

Jonas, more sensitive. Talk about the antihero's journey.

"It was a good show," Yossi says simply, his hands clasped serenely on the table in front of him. He is calm, confident.

God.

For her part, Reena says nothing, just shifts in her seat and twists her flexi-straw against the lip of the largest glass of Coke I've ever seen. So far, she hasn't taken so much as a sip.

"What? Is it Diet?" I tease, reaching across the table to poke at her.

Her mouth smiles—barely—but her eyes don't.

I'm going down. Time to switch tactics. The direct approach worked with Mom and Dad, so I decide to take another stab at it. I am the Master of All Things Obvious.

"The party was kind of intense," I offer finally.

"Yup." Jonas nods.

"I'm thinking..." What am I thinking? "I'm thinking that we are awesome, that we kick total ass, but that maybe we need, like, a little break. Some time off."

Yeah, that's what I'm thinking.

Once upon a time, I would have gladly opted to skewer

my heart with a sharpened drumstick rather than take any time away from the Tribe, but for now it feels like the right call. Like if we don't do it, we'll all choke on the stale air of the Gluck racquetball court.

For a moment no one says anything. Then Reena takes a quiet sip of her soda at last.

"The racquetball court was starting to feel kinda cramped, right?"

Right.

"But, like, it's just a break, right, man? I mean, we're still gonna have a band, aren't we, Ari?" Jonas looks up at me, and for the first time since maybe the fourth grade he looks like he's waiting on me. Waiting on *me*, for something.

I give up. My mind has officially been blown. We've entered Bizarro World.

"Principal Friedel came up to me in the library yesterday at lunch," Yossi says. "Student Council is starting to plan the Purim Prom. They wanted to know if we'd play."

I have to admit, I'm intrigued—but not sure where this next "gig" would fit in our grand scheme of spending less time together as a band for the immediate future.

"I told her we'd do it."

I could not be more shocked if Yossi had just announced that he was running off to join the Church of Scientology. *Yossi* confirmed our gig? *Yossi?* Since when did Yossi become our point person?

"Are they going to pay us?" Jonas asks. It's a good question, actually.

Yossi shrugs. "Kosher pizza. Punch."

"I like punch," Reena says, perking up. "And Purim isn't until April. So we'd have a little time before we'd have to start practicing again. And we can all take winter break to, you know, chill out a little bit. Relax."

She's right, of course. I'm a big punch person myself. A fan of the punch. This really could be the perfect thing for us. I straighten in my seat, open my mouth to say as much, but Yossi beats me to it.

"Well then, that's perfect."

And it's like the word of God, that. What can you do but go along with it?

• • •

Here's the thing: a most people think the word *mensch* is about being righteous, being good people. But strictly defined, all it actually means is "a man." That's it. Just a person, no matter how you slice it. So what I guess some of us don't realize—what *I* sure never realized, anyway—is that all it takes, then, to be quality, to be a solid citizen (Jewish or otherwise), is to know yourself. To know what you stand for.

I am not a mensch, yet. But I'm trying.

• • •

Yossi hits the men's room, and Jonas goes up to the cashier to take care of our check. The expanse of Formica tabletop between Reena and me yawns. Reena yawns, rubs at her eyes, then suddenly crosses them at me.

God, she's cool.

"How's Kevin?" I ask.

She stares at me for a minute. I deserve that.

"You're an idiot," she says eventually.

I deserve that, too.

"Are you . . . "

Okay, here's something I know about myself, something that I stand for: I stand for hanging out with Reena. More. A lot, really, if that's, you know, on the menu. "What are you doing tomorrow?"

"It's Shabbos," she says, sweeping her index finger side to side in a *tsk*-y sort of gesture.

"Duh." This gets a small giggle. It's all the encouragement I need. "I meant *after*."

She shrugs. "Hanging out with an idiot?"

Works for me.

She holds my gaze for a beat, then takes a big, healthy slurp of her soda. "You never did tell me how you managed to get your parents to consider the possibility of NYU."

"Oh." I wave my hand dismissively. "We went online, looked at some pictures and stuff. Did you know that NYU has a *huge* Hillel center? Seriously. It takes up, like, two city blocks."

She shakes her head, laughing. "I can't believe we missed that on our whirlwind tour. But okay, sure. That's your angle, right there." She nods, mostly to herself, I think. "Kosher. That's totally kosher."

Amen, right?

FOUR OF A KIND
BEATING AS ONE
YO LA TENGO
KINKS
The Who
LIVE AT LEEDS
WELL, WHADDYA SAY BOYS? LET'S SEE WHAT YOU GOT.
CBGB
OH MAN, WHY DID I GO ALL IN?!

BECAUSE, EUGENE, YOU'RE A TERRIBLE POKER PLAYER.
THE STOOGES
RAW POWER

HEY MAN, WHO BROUGHT THE UNO DECK? AND WHO SAID "HEY, LET'S PLAY UNO, I DON'T REALLY KNOW ANYTHING ABOUT POKER."?

EUGENE, YOU'RE A DISGRACE. NOW QUIET ALL OF YEZ WHILE I DEAL.
AD HERE
SPIN
WHAP!
WHAT ARE YOU GUYS WAITING FOR, SIMCHAS TORAH?! THE CROWD'S GETTING RESTLESS! YOU'RE ON!

HEY, WHEN IS SIMCHAS TORAH THIS YEAR, ANYWAY?
UH, OCTOBER, I THINK.
STAGE →

YEAH!
WOOHOO!
GOOD EVENING LADIES AND GENTLEMEN
SO PUNK ROCK!!
THANKS MOM!

MOM?!
YOUR REPORT CARD! A+ IN CALC-
ULUS? THAT'S SO... PUNK ROCK!
ISN'T... ISN'T THAT
WHAT YOU KIDS SAY?
DEATH TO THE
PIXIES

NO.

I CAN SAY WITH COMPLETE CONFIDENCE
THAT NOT A SINGLE ONE OF MY FRIENDS
HAS EVER USED THAT EXPRESSION. DID
BEN TELL YOU TO SAY THAT? I TOLD YOU
MOM, ALWAYS COME TO ME FIRST.

WELL THEN WHAT EXPRESSION WOULD YOUR FRIENDS USE TO DESCRIBE YOUR EXCELLENT ACADEMIC ACHIEVEMENT?
ROTHKO
MOM
JEANS
WELL ... SOMETIMES THEY SAY... KOSHER.
REALLY?
KOSHER! HAH! THAT'S GREAT. I'LL HAVE TO TELL YOUR FATHER THAT ONE. HE'LL LOVE IT.

HEY GERALD, DID YOU SEE ARI'S REPORT CARD? IT'S KOSHER! ALSO BEN CAME IN SECOND IN HIS CLASS SPELLING BEE. HOW KOSHER IS THAT? HEY, YOU KNOW WHAT ELSE IS KOSHER? DINNER! HAH! HEY GERALD, ARE YOU GETTING THIS? KOSHER!

S**T

I SHOULD HAVE JUST LET HER USE THAT PUNK ROCK THING.

GLOSSARY OF JEWISH, MUSICAL AND OTHERWISE ESOTERIC TERMS*

- **BOKER TOV**- HEBREW FOR 'GOOD MORNING'
- **CONSERVATIVE JEWISH MOVEMENT**- WIDESPREAD BRANCH OF JUDAISM WHICH SEEKS TO PRESERVE THE FUNDAMENTALS OF TRADITIONAL JEWISH PRACTICE WHILE ACKNOWLEDGING THE NEED TO REINTERPRET ASPECTS OF THIS PRACTICE TO MEET THE CHALLENGES OF THE MODERN WORLD.
- **FENDER**- LEGENDARY MANUFACTURER OF ELECTRIC GUITARS SINCE THE 1940'S. THE FENDER **STRATOCASTER** MIGHT BE THE MOST POPULAR GUITAR IN THE HISTORY OF ROCKDOM. THAT'S RIGHT... ROCKDOM.
- **HADASSAH**- JEWISH WOMEN'S CHARITABLE ORGANIZATION. THE NAME HADASSAH DERIVES FROM THAT OF A BIBLICAL HEROINE. WHICH, YOU KNOW, PROPS TO THEM FOR FINDING THAT NAME BECAUSE I'VE LOOKED THROUGH THE BIBLE AND IT'S A PRETTY DUDE-CENTRIC READ.
- **HANNUKAH**- HOLIDAY ON WHICH WE REMEMBER THE JEWISH VICTORY OVER THE **SELEUCID EMPIRE** WAY BACK IN THE DAY. TODAY THE STEREOTYPICAL JEW IS BOOKISH AND NOT SO PHYSICALLY ADEPT BUT APPARENTLY ONCE UPON A TIME WE WERE CAPABLE OF DISHING OUT SOME SERIOUS WHOOPASS. **(FIG. 1)**
- **HAVA NAGILA**- TRADITIONAL JEWISH FOLK SONG OFTEN DANCED TO AT WEDDINGS, BAR AND BAT MITZVAHS AND OTHER FESTIVITIES. THE DANCE THAT ACCOMPANIES THIS NUMBER IS, OF COURSE **THE HORA** **(FIG. 2)** WHICH BEGINS WHEN 3 OR MORE OVER-ZEALOUS PARTY GOERS JOIN HANDS TO FORM A RING AND START MOVING IN CIRCLES AT A PACE THAT MAY OR MAY NOT APPROXIMATE THE TEMPO ESTABLISHED BY THE MUSICIANS. AS MORE PARTY GOERS JOIN THE RING THE DANCE BECOMES INCREASINGLY UNSTEADY. MORE OFTEN THAN NOT, AT LEAST ONE PARTICIPANT (USUALLY SOMEONE'S DRUNK GREAT-UNCLE) LOSES HIS GRASP ON HIS NEIGHBOR'S HAND AND VEER'S OFF INTO SPACE WITH A CHAIN OF PARTICIPANTS IN TOW, BASICALLY INVITING CERTAIN CHAOS ONTO THE DANCE FLOOR. A MAGNIFICENT DEMONSTRATION OF THE ABSENCE OF PHYSICAL COORDINATION FROM THE JEWISH GENE POOL.
- **KABBALAH**- OLD, ESOTERIC AND EXTREMELY INTELLECTUALLY DEMANDING FORM OF JEWISH MYSTICISM WITH SHADOWY ORIGINS IN THE MIDDLE AGES. ALSO A CASUAL PASTIME OF MADONNA'S.
- **KLEZMER**- ETHNICALLY JEWISH STYLE OF MUSIC FEATURING UPBEAT SYNCOPATED TEMPOS AND SHORT MEN WITH BEARDS PLAYING THE ACCORDION WITH OLD-WORLD ABANDON **(FIG 3)**
- **KOSHER**- PERMISSABLE TO EAT ACCORDING TO JEWISH LAW. ALSO, MORE RECENTLY, SLANG

FIG. 1: THE JEWISH MALE, THEN AND NOW

FIG 2: THE LIFE (AND DEATH) OF A HORA

A- A PIONEERING MINORITY OF GUESTS ABANDON THEIR SEATING ASSIGNMENTS TO FORM A CLOCKWISE-ROTATING RING ON THE DANCE FLOOR.

B- MORE GUESTS JOIN IN, CLASPING HANDS WITH THOSE TO EITHER SIDE OF THEM. THE RING IS COMPLETE. THE HORA HAS OFFICIALLY BEGUN.

C- MOMENTARILY DISTRACTED BY A YOUNG, ATTRACTIVE MEMBER OF THE WAIT STAFF, UNCLE SEYMOUR INADVERTANTLY BREAKS RANK WITH THE RING

D- BIRTH OF THE SPLINTER RING AS UNCLE SEYMOUR'S CLOSEST NIEGHBORS ARE DRAGGED HAPLESSLY ALONG ON HIS RECKLESS COURSE

E- MULTIPLICATION OF SPLINTER RINGS AS MASS CONFUSION SETS IN AND MORE GUESTS FLOOD THE DANCE FLOOR BECAUSE 'HEY, IT'S LOOKING PRETTY CRAZY OUT THERE!'

F- REAL ESTATE CRISIS ON DANCE FLOOR FORCES ALL RINGS INTO GRACELESS AMOEBA-LIKE FORMS. BAND SWITCHES TO A MEDLEY OF MOTOWN HITS.

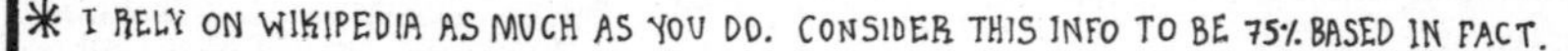

* I RELY ON WIKIPEDIA AS MUCH AS YOU DO. CONSIDER THIS INFO TO BE 75% BASED IN FACT.

FOR 'OK' OR 'COOL'. BUT, REALLY, IF YOU DON'T KNOW THAT AT THIS POINT I'D WAGER THAT YOU HAVEN'T READ THIS BOOK VERY CAREFULLY AND I CERTAINLY DIDN'T WRITE IT SO YOU COULD SKIP RIGHT TO THE END. GO BACK AND READ MAN! **(FIG 4)**

- **MAIMONEDES**– 13th-CENTURY JEWISH SCHOLAR AND PHYSICIAN. PRETTY SMART GUY I'M TOLD. LIKED HUMMUS.
- **MANISCHEWITZ**– POPULAR BRAND OF KOSHER FOODSTUFFS BEST KNOWN FOR ITS SIGNATURE 'WINE'. I PUT 'WINE' IN QUOTATION MARKS BECAUSE IT TASTES MORE LIKE GRAPE JUICE WITH A SHOT OF NAIL POLISH REMOVER. RARELY FOUND IN THE CELLARS OF SERIOUS WINE AFICIONADOS, THE CLASSIC MANISCHEWITZ RED IS NONETHELESS GOOD FOR TAKING THE EDGE OFF AFTER A LONG SATURDAY MORNING IN **SYNAGOGUE** (SEE 'SYNAGOGUE' BELOW)
- **MATZOH**– UNLEAVENED BREAD. A STAPLE OF THE RESTRICTIVE DIETARY LAWS IMPLEMENTED ON THE 8 DAYS OF **PASSOVER** (SEE 'PASSOVER' BELOW). CONSUMPTION ALLEVIATES MOST CASES OF CHRONIC DIARRHEA.
- **MITZVAH**– TRANSLATES FROM HEBREW TO **'COMMANDMENT'**. BUT WE'RE NOT JUST TALKING ABOUT THE TEN THAT MOST PEOPLE KNOW AND LOVE. IN JUDAISM THERE ARE 613 'MITZVOT'. I COULDN'T NAME THEM ALL BUT I'M PRETTY SURE YOU CAN COVER AT LEAST 10% OF THEM SIMPLY BY NOT BEING A TOTAL A**HOLE **(FIG. 5)**. THE TERM 'MITZVAH' IS OFTEN USED TO DESCRIBE ANY PIOUS ACT THAT GOD WOULD PROBABLY APPROVE OF.
- **PASSOVER**– 8-DAY HOLIDAY IN REMEMBRANCE OF THE ANCIENT ISRAELITES' EXODUS OUT OF EGYPT. ON THE FIRST 2 NIGHTS OF PASSOVER JEWS ATTEND A RITUAL MEAL CALLED **A SEDER** DURING WHICH WE ARE MANDATED TO RETELL THE STORY OF HOW GOD TOOK US OUT OF EGYPT, WHERE WE WERE SLAVES, AND INTO THE PROMISED LAND. GOD LIKES HEARING US TELL THIS STORY WHICH IS KIND OF LIKE HAVING AN ARMY BUDDY WHO'S ALWAYS ASKING YOU TO REMIND HIM OF THAT TIME HE SAVED YOUR A** IN 'NAM.
- **PURIM**– HOLIDAY CELEBRATING THE JEWS' EMANCIPATION FROM THE CONNIVING HANDS OF AN AMBITIOUS MEMBER OF THE PERSIAN ROYAL COURT. IT'S A LIGHT-HEARTED HOLIDAY WITH A MASQUERADE COMPONENT SO OUR PARENTS AND TEACHERS ENCOURAGE US TO SEE IT AS A JEWISH ALTERNATIVE TO HALLOWEEN. HOWEVER NO CANDY + NO JACKOLANTERNS + NO HORROR MOVIES = NOT EVEN REMOTELY LIKE HALLOWEEN.
- **ROSH HASHANA**– THE JEWISH NEW YEAR. KIND OF LIKE REGULAR NEW YEARS EXCEPT LESS WITH THE CHAMPAGNE AND MORE WITH THE PRAYING.
- **SHABBOS**– (SEE 'SHOMER SHABBOS' BELOW)
- **SHOFAR**– A RAM'S HORN USED AS A SORT OF WIND INSTRUMENT IN JEWISH RITUALS ON ROSH HASHANA (SEE 'ROSH HASHANA' ABOVE). WHEN BLOWN PROPERLY THE SHOFAR MAKES A PRETTY HAUNTING SOUND, ONE CAPABLE OF STIRRING FEELINGS OF RELIGIOSITY IN THE MOST CYNICAL OF PEOPLE. I CAN SEE WHY IT'S GOD'S FAVORITE INSTRUMENT **(FIG 6)**
- **SHOMER SHABBOS**– 'OBSERVANT OF THE SABBATH'. THE JEWISH SABBATH FALLS EVERY WEEK FROM SUNDOWN ON FRIDAY TO SUNDOWN ON SATURDAY. ON IT, WE ARE COMMANDED TO REST AS GOD RESTED ON THE 7th DAY OF CREATION. FOR MANY JEWS THIS MEANS REFRAINING FROM ANY SORT OF CREATIVE ACT.

FIG 3: TYPICAL KLEZMER BAND

FIG 4: CONTEMPORARY USES FOR 'KOSHER'

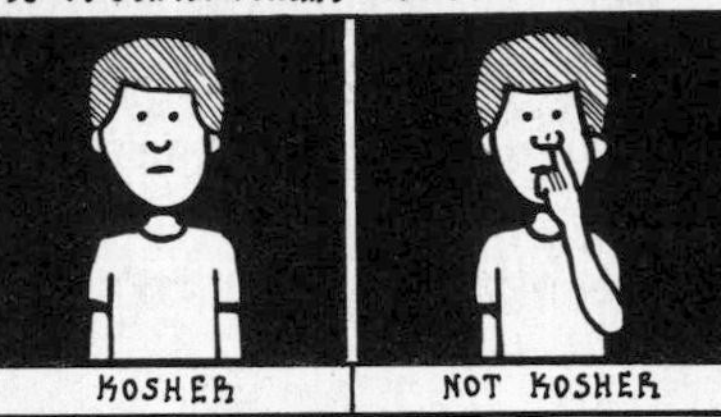

FIG 5: THE 613 COMMANDMENTS

THIS INCLUDES A PROHIBITION AGAINST LIGHTING FIRES WHICH MOST MODERN BRANCHES OF JUDAISM EXTEND TO MEAN TRIGGERING ANY SORT OF IGNITION, FROM TURNING ON THE TV TO STARTING A CAR ENGINE. THIS IS WHY YOSSI WILL NOT DRIVE ON SATURDAYS.

- **SIMCHAS TORAH**- HOLIDAY CELEBRATING THE END OF THE YEARLY CYCLE OF TORAH READINGS (SEE **'TORAH'** BELOW) JEWS PERFORM WEEKLY. MORE SIGNIFICANTLY, THE ONLY HOLIDAY WHERE CANDY APPLES ARE DOLED OUT TO YOUNG CHILDREN WHO ARE ALREADY HIGH STRUNG FROM A DAY SPENT IN SYNAGOGUE (SEE **'SYNAGOGUE'** BELOW)
- **SKA**- MUSICAL GENRE, JAMAICAN IN ORIGIN, COMPONENTS OF WHICH WERE APPROPRIATED BY BRITISH PUNK BANDS IN THE LATE 1970'S. SKA IS CHARACTERIZED BY FAST, DANCEABLE, SYNCHOPATED BEATS AND ASSOCIATED-FOR REASONS BEYOND ME- WITH BLACK & WHITE CHECKERED CLOTHING.
- **SYNAGOGUE**- KIND OF LIKE CHURCH... BUT FOR JEWS.
- **TEMPLE**- WORD OFTEN USED IN LIEU OF 'SYNAGOGUE.' BUT TO ME 'TEMPLE' SOUNDS LIKE THE PLACE ONE WOULD GO TO WORSHIP THE BLOODLUSTING GOD OF FIRE WHICH- I CAN ASSURE YOU IN SPITE OF SOME NASTY RUMORS- WE JEWS DO NOT. **(FIG. 7)**
- **TORAH**- THE SACRED BOOK OF THE JEWS. ALSO HELD SACRED BY **CHRISTIANS** AND **MUSLIMS.** ALL 3 RELIGIONS HAVE DIVERGING OPINIONS ABOUT THE POINT OF THE BOOK, WHETHER OR NOT IT'S AS GOOD OR IMPORTANT AS OTHER BOOKS THAT CAME LATER, ETC. SO BASICALLY THE ENTIRE VIOLENT, BLOODY HISTORY OF WESTERN RELIGION IS A BOOK CLUB THAT KINDA GOT OUTTA CONTROL. SO LET'S JUST SORT OUT OUR EMOTIONS, MOVE ONTO THE LATEST JK ROWLING (YEAH, SHE CAME OUT WITH NUMBER 7 WHILE WE WERE BUSY ARGUING) AND JUST CALM THE EFF DOWN.
- **TRAIF**- 'NOT KOSHER' AND HERE I MEAN 'KOSHER' IN ITS ORIGINAL SENSE. IF YOU ARE A JEW AND SOMETHING IS TRAIF YOU CANNOT EAT SAID SOMETHING EVEN THOUGH SAID SOMETHING IS PROBABLY TASTIER THAN WHAT YOU'RE EATING.
- **TRIBE**- SLANG TERM USED BY JEWS TO REFER TO THEMSELVES AS A COMMUNITY. PROBABLY ORIGINATES IN THE FACT THAT WE ALL DESCEND FROM THE ONE ISRAELITE TRIBE OUT OF 12 THAT DIDN'T HAVE ITS ASS HANDED TO IT BY THE **ASSYRIAN EMPIRE** 3000 YEARS AGO.
- **TZEDAKKAH**- HEBREW WORD FOR CHARITY. A 'TZEDAKKAH BOX' IS A CONTAINER FOR THE COLLECTION OF CHARITABLE DONATIONS.
- **YARMULKE**- CLOTH HEADCOVERING WORN BY JEWISH MALES (AND SOME FEMALES). SO IF YOU WERE WONDERING ABOUT THE LITTLE OVALS ON PEOPLES' HEADS IN MY CARTOONS, THERE'S YOUR ANSWER.
- **YOM KIPPUR**- JEWISH DAY OF ATONEMENT ON WHICH WE FAST IN ORDER TO REFLECT ON OUR SINS. PROBLEM IS, WITH NO FOOD IN MY STOMACH I CAN'T REFLECT MUCH PAST AN EGGO WAFFLE.
- **ZIONISM**- THIS IS A FAIRLY LOADED TERM THAT MEANS DIFFERENT THINGS TO DIFFERENT PEOPLE. BRIEFLY, ZIONISM IS THE BELIEF IN THE JEWS' RIGHT TO THE STATE OF ISRAEL. TO MANY IN THE JEWISH COMMUNITY IT IS AN INNOCUOUS, EVEN POSITIVE CONCEPT GROUNDED IN THE BELIEF THAT A JEWISH STATE IS FUNDAMENTAL TO THE CONTINUED SECURITY OF THE JEWISH PEOPLE. OTHERS SEE ZIONISM AS AN OPPRESSIVE FORM OF IMPERIALISM CONNECTED TO THE ONGOING PLIGHT OF THE **PALESTINIANS.** MY OWN UNDERSTANDING OF ZIONISM IS LIMITED SO I'LL STOP WRITING BEFORE I ACCIDENTALLY PISS OFF ANYONE ON EITHER SIDE OF THE ARGUMENT.

FIG 6: GOD WITH HIS SHOFAR, GREENWICH VILLAGE, NEW YORK CITY, 1963

FIG 7: SYNAGOGUE VS. TEMPLE

David Ostow was born and raised in South Orange, New Jersey. As a teenager, he played guitar in a garage band that managed to come in last place in a battle of the bands held at the local Jewish Community Center. When the band thing didn't work out he went off to college and eventually decided to train as an architect, which is why he draws buildings better than people. He currently lives in Hoboken, New Jersey, works as a designer in New York City, and sleeps anywhere no one will bother him.

Micol Ostow has published over thirty-five works for children, tweens, and teens. Her first original hardcover novel, *Emily Goldberg Learns to Salsa*, was named a New York Public Library Books for the Teen Age selection. Like David, Micol endured thirteen years of Jewish day school and came out the other end with enough affection intact to inspire an entire book set in that unique, quirky, and quasi-unbelievable world. Unlike David, she does not draw or play music. She does, however, sing in the shower—and totally rocks it out. She lives in Manhattan with her film-maker fiancé and a persnickety French Bulldog named Bridget Jones. Visit Micol at www.micolostow.com.